TAROT WITCH

A SEASHELL COVE PARANORMAL MYSTERY

T. THORN COYLE

"Carol thought I should know what?" I finally asked, plucking *Stories of Ghostly Encounters* by Harold Dean from the shelf and slotting it back in its proper place.

Tracy raked one pink Converse high top across the carpet. "My mom wanted you to know that her athame is missing."

My blood ran cold.

1

———

I t was a glorious June day in Seashell Cove, and we were barreling toward Summer Solstice. Tourists walked by the book-filled windows of my shop, The Widening Gyre, dripping ice cream, while across the street, adults dragged children away from the giant T-Rex replica Tetris had recently installed outside his curio and fossil shop, Ancient Treasures.

Rhiannon perched in one of the sunny display windows, washing a furry black paw in front of a stack of historical mysteries. An older couple paused outside the window to coo in her direction. Cats are good for business. Even though she was strong willed and a bit cranky, her presence alone meant Rhiannon earned her keep. Though, since I had recently discovered—through a strange turn of events—that she can talk in language intelligible to non-cat ears?[1] Turns out Rhiannon has opinions. Strong ones. Constantly. I sometimes wish I'd never figured it out.

She ignored the couple. Typical. It wasn't that

Rhiannon didn't like attention—she did—but if you weren't offering head scratches or food, mostly she didn't bother.

"Sarah!" Tracy burst through the front door, blond hair flying, setting the bells clattering. Dark-haired Tabitha was hot on her sneakered heels. Both teens wore Converse All Stars; Tracy's were pink and Tabitha's black. Before meeting the dynamic duo, I hadn't even known those kicks were back in style.

I looked up from the customer I was helping, a precocious twelve-year-old kid—Ash Hamamoto— whose father had dropped him off while he ran errands down Main. Parent and child had recently moved to town, and seemed nice. But then, I like almost anyone who loves reading. It's a sign of good character. I didn't yet know the Hamamotos' story, but in Seashell Cove? I was sure I'd find out soon enough. If it was the slow season, the gossip mill would have churned its info my way by now.

Lucky for Ash's father, it was tourist season and the locals were preoccupied with squirreling away money for the slow winter months.

Ash wore jeans, sneakers, and a manga T-shirt with bright, sharply drawn characters I didn't recognize. He had delicate features and dark hair cut in a brush cut that reminded me of a hedgehog. In between browsing the bookshelves, Ash had been telling me about his love of D&D. I was going to have to introduce him to my big bear of a geeky boyfriend, Stefon.

"Just a minute, Tracy. I'll be right with you." I gave both teens a firm *Don't bring whatever it is into the shop in front of customers* look.

"We'll wait back in the paranormal section," Tabitha said, grabbing her best friend by the shoulders and steering her down the aisle where Biff the ghost hovered. Biff loved the teens and always materialized more when they were around.

I turned back to Ash, who had two books in hand.

"Did you like the Ursula K. LeGuin book? Or did you prefer the Kwame Mbalia?"

Ash shrugged. "I liked them both. But Dad says I should stick with used books today, so I guess I'll try this one."

He held up a battered copy of *Eragon*.

"Dragons are always a good choice," I said. "Let's get you rung up."

I could feel the teens practically vibrating at the back of the shop. Out of sight was definitely not out of mind with those two. Now that Tracy was coming into her witchy powers, and Tabitha was training in psychic skills, both teens broadcast like *whoa*. I needed to have a talk with them about shielding practice, clearly. Maybe Tracy's mother, Carol, could help with that. Uncle Cyrus was supposed to be mentoring them, but hadn't been around much lately.

I sighed. We needed to set up a local training consortium or something. I had no interest in doing it myself. I really needed to ping Cyrus.

"You okay?" Ash asked, face scrunched into a furrow.

He must have heard my sigh. Or he was a budding empath. Great. Another malleable young person who would likely need my help soon. I really didn't want this added to my pile.

Ash's dad walked in as if summoned. A Japanese-American man in his mid-forties, he was neatly dressed in a black T-shirt, blue jeans, and sneakers. His hair was stick straight, short, and as dark as Tabitha's and he wore stylish green-framed glasses.

"Dad! I'm getting this one, okay?"

Jerry Hamamoto nodded and smiled at his child, but his face looked pinched with worry. Was money that tight? Or was it something else? Seashell Cove used to have a library, but it had closed a few years back from lack of funding. As if books weren't more important than...whatever else our town council decided to spend money on.

At any rate, I couldn't imagine being a single parent to a gender non-conforming tween in a small town was easy. Especially as newcomers. Neither of them had said anything directly, but it seemed pretty clear to me that Ash was trans.

Good on Dad for supporting him.

"You know what?" I said, drawing Ash's gaze back my way. "Why don't I give this to you in exchange for writing up some shelf talkers for the store?"

"Shelf talkers?"

"You know, like those." I pointed to the small rectangles of paper taped to some of the bookshelves. They were covered with neat printing, mini-reviews, mostly written by my assistant, Duncan, or myself. But a few still held my father's crabbed writing. I couldn't bear to throw those in the recycling. Not yet.

"You just have to write a few sentences telling people what you liked about the book, but without giving away the story. And print it out neatly."

Mr. Hamamoto looked relieved. "Ash has been studying calligraphy lately, so that's perfect! Isn't it, Ash?"

Ash nodded, and turned back to the book.

Jerry glanced back at me. "Thank you," he mouthed.

I shrugged. "This will be a big help. We need more reviews in the middle grade and YA sections. And Ash, if you want to trade it in for another used book to review, just let me know! I might need your help with other display signs around the shop, too."

Finally I got parent and child bustled out of the shop. I peered down a couple of aisles to make sure I hadn't missed any lingering customers, and followed the sound of the teens hushed, excited voices to the very back of the store.

They were huddled over a book, standing in the aisle near the comfy chair shoved in the back corner between two bookcases.

"What's up?"

Both heads whipped toward me, as if I'd startled them.

"Tracy's mom thought you should know..." Tabitha started, then paused, winding a lock of dark, straight hair around one finger. Tabitha was Chinese American and looked it. She was in Goth mode as usual, dressing like a teen witch, which was amusing to me, partially because I had been a Goth teen myself, and partially because although Tracy was the hereditary witch of the pair, she was dressed in blue jeans and a pale blue T-shirt with a cartoon ghost carrying a load of books. The T-shirt was the latest scheme the teenagers were using to bring more cash into the store: T-shirts advertising the presence of Biff the ghost.

I hated it, but had to admit the girls were probably right.

In contrast, Tabitha wore black jeans and a black T-shirt with a hot pink pentacle on the front.

"Carol thought I should know what?" I finally asked, plucking *Stories of Ghostly Encounters* by Harold Dean from the shelf and slotting it back in its proper place.

Tracy raked one pink Converse high top across the carpet. "My mom wanted you to know that her athame is missing."

My blood ran cold.

An athame is a witch's ritual knife. It represents her will and intention and is energetically linked to her soul by breath and magic.

This was bad. Very bad.

"Is she sure? She didn't just leave it in an unlikely place?"

Both teens rolled their eyes.

"As if," Tabitha said.

Fair enough. No witch or warlock—or magician, for that matter—would misplace something as important as a magical tool.

So where in the nine worlds had it gone?

Rhiannon sauntered to the back and yawned.

"Maybe it's at the Kelpie," I said. "You know how much the ghosts there like magic things."

The Historic Kelpie was Seashell Cove's favorite haunted inn. Unlike me, the owner, Liam, capitalized on the fact that the place was lousy with ghosts. And dancing ones at that. We all had recent experience with what happened when one of the ghosts decided they wanted something.

I looked at Tracy, who shrugged. "As far as I know, Mom hasn't been to The Kelpie lately."

Meaning, not since we'd solved the case of the dead opera singer.

"Tell Carol I'll meet with her this evening. My back-yard. Bring snacks. I don't have time to go to the store today."

I would provide the drinks, but the two teenagers would mow through any snacks I had hidden away.

"We wanted to do some more research," Tabitha said, nose already buried in yet another book.

"Okay. You can stay here, but Rhiannon and I have to get back to work."

Which was a good thing. Maybe, just maybe, The Widening Gyre was turning its finances around, even without the T-shirt sales.

2

I clomped down the back steps from the kitchen, balancing a tray filled with cups, glasses, and a pitcher of lemonade. Stefon followed behind, carrying a small cooler of flavored fizzy waters.

"You sure we shouldn't bring out snacks, babe?"

After setting the tray on the round, metal table near the back of the garden, I turned. The sight of my large, tall boyfriend, dark skin shining in the evening sun, still took my breath away. If we didn't have a gaggle of people arriving soon, I would pull that bearded face down to mine and kiss him until he picked me up and carried me back into the house.

I said he was large, didn't I? A knight with the Society for Medieval Anachronism, Stefon had the muscles to easily pick up tall, size-sixteen me. It was one of the many things I loved about him. That, his smile, and his brain. Did I mention he was also a computer programmer and gamer geek?

Case in point, this evening his dark gray jeans were topped by an *It's How I Roll* T-shirt featuring an orange, twenty-sided die that matched the color of his orange sneakers.

"Sarah! You back here?" That was Tabitha's voice. Drat. No time for that kiss.

"I hope you brought snacks!" I called back, grinning at Stefon. He laughed, set the cooler down near the table, and grabbed a few more folding chairs to add to the set that came with the table.

A tiny slice of rolling ocean, white caps gleaming, peeked out between my neighbor's back hedge and the house next door. It wasn't much, but most places in my neighborhood didn't have any ocean view at all. It was the only reason my parents could have afforded the bungalow in the first place.

Carol followed after the teens. She carried a bottle of wine, and had a large gray leather purse slung over one shoulder. Both the teens hoisted cotton tote bags filled with what I was sure were their favorite snacks. I was amazingly happy to see them, which was strange, all things considered. There was a time when I thought the teens were a pain in the butt. But not only were they smart, funny, and kind, they had proven to be very helpful.

Both of them worked a lot on researching the cases that fell in my lap as a magical Justice. And the more Tracy trained in magic, the more helpful they both would become.

Carol walked across the small patchy bit of grass in between the shrubs and other plants that bordered my small back garden. She was a striking witch with long blond hair just a shade darker than Tracy's. She was more slender than I am, with the kind of figure people used to call "boyish," and looked cool and crisp in dark jeans and a pale peach T-shirt with a silver necklace glinting at her throat. Her left hand sported a moonstone ring.

She smiled, but I could tell that worry dogged her heels.

"Thanks for having us over, Sarah," she said. "Nice to see you, Stefon."

"Nice to see you too," my boyfriend replied, helping the teens carry the bags into the kitchen.

Turns out it's really nice having a boyfriend. That was something I never thought I'd say after Cecilia and I broke up, and then Dad got sick. But now, Cecilia was my best friend and had her own partner, and I had someone I was rapidly starting to think was long-term-partner material myself.

It wasn't that I hadn't wanted someone after Cecilia, and it wasn't that I hadn't dated around. A lot. But taking care of the bookshop and my father while he was dying had been more than enough for me.

I smiled. Stefon's persistence had won out.

Standing in my backyard, with friends and accomplices gathering, I was glad to have someone who had my back for the larger things in life, and also with simple things like helping me host a small gathering.

"It's the least I could do," I said to Carol. "When was the last time you saw the knife?"

She shook her head and frowned. "If it's all the

same to you, I'd rather wait and tell the whole tale at once. Once Stefon comes back... And didn't you say some other people were coming? Cecilia? And is Delta coming?"

Delta Crabbit was another local witch who had helped out with a few cases once I'd ruled her out as a suspect in one of them. Luckily, she didn't hold that against me.

Oh, and her best friend was a gnome named Preston. Gotta love Seashell Cove, right?

I took the bottle of wine off Carol's hands. A screw top. No bottle opener needed. "No Delta, but Cecilia and Toby wanted to come for some reason."

I grabbed a couple of the smaller cups. No wine-glasses needed either. I wasn't usually a person who relied on alcohol for more than having a bit of fun, but it looked like Carol could use some outside help to calm her nerves. I poured the chilled golden liquid into hand-thrown ceramic cups, one green, one deep blue, then put the bottle into the cooler.

"Let's have a seat," I said. There was really no time to enjoy the ocean air, the quiet garden, or the wine. I exhaled slowly, trying to ramp myself down none-theless.

As soon as we sat down, Cecilia and Toby burst through the back gate.

"What's going on?" Cecilia asked, fuchsia hair bobbing around her shoulders. My ex-girlfriend was a colorful, Asian-American whirlwind. "Did we miss anything?" Her skinny arm dragged at Toby's hand. I had to grin at that. They were quite a pair. The auto mechanic and the hob. The bright-as-stained-glass cis woman, and the non-binary, hope-you-don't-notice-me hob. And by hob, I mean a domestic fae being that loves nothing more than to make a hearth a home. That means Cecilia has a super-clean kitchen, lucky duck. Toby was also handy with plants in the garden and helped out Mr. Vargas with his landscaping business during the busy season.

As short as my ex-girlfriend is, Toby is even shorter. They have a slight frame and dusky brown skin that matches their sturdy brown work pants. Today, for a bit of contrast, they wore an olive-green T-shirt. Cecilia wore sparkle-pink Doc Martens, but instead of her usual black with rainbow accents, the bright shoes were topped by white jeans and a white T-shirt. In honor of summer, I guess. And the fact that she had to wear greasy overalls at work.

I'd probably wear white in that case, too. Except that I'm sometimes prone to catching things on the broad shelf that is my heaving bosom. White doesn't always work out so well in that case.

"Carol will tell us once Stefon and the girls come back out."

"Fair enough," Cecilia said. "Toby, you remember Carol?"

Carol raised her cup in the hob's direction. "Thanks for coming. Both of you."

"Sure," Cecilia replied. "We have some intel of our own. Not sure if it's related yet."

Toby just shrugged and ran a free hand down their thighs, wiping off sweat. Hobs are pretty private and shy, and Toby's super-introverted.

Finally, Stefon and the teens came back out with an array of chips and crackers in my father's old blue and yellow mixing bowls. And thankfully—because clearly Carol had gone shopping and not just the teens—there was also an array of cheese, carrot sticks, and a tub of hummus. My stomach growled. I'd had salad for dinner, which was really not enough for me. But I had been too keyed up to eat much after work and figured I'd be chowing down on snacks. Once everyone was settled and the teens were happily munching away, I snagged a piece of cheddar.

"Okay, Carol. Tell us what you got." I shoved the cheese in my mouth and chewed, waiting, as the blond-haired witch took another sip of wine.

She frowned into her cup and then set it on the metal table with a click.

"Okay," she said, "here goes."

Tabitha elbowed Tracy to stop crunching.

"Sorry," Tracy mumbled, grabbing a paper napkin to wipe the grease from her hands. Carol just waited. But it wasn't as if she was waiting for us to settle down. Her eyes had a faraway look in them, the way witches' eyes sometimes got when their spirits traveled elsewhere. Or elsewhen.

"I'd done my full moon ritual, as usual, then snuffed the candles, tidied the altar, and resheathed my athame."

I took a sip of the crisp white wine. I really wanted some carrots and hummus, but didn't want to break the spell. But Carol had just stopped speaking. As if she was done.

"Mom," Tracy prodded. "Just tell them what happened next."

Carol shook as if startled back into the present moment. She leaned forward and grabbed a baby carrot, then looked at it as if she'd never seen one before.

What the heck was going on?

3

———

"**M**om!"

Carol's head snapped toward her daughter. "What?"

Her voice sounded truly bewildered, as if she had no idea how strange she was acting. I mean, before I realized Carol was a witch, she just seemed like a normal human to me. You know? Minivan. Beautiful daughter with a great friend. Regular bookkeeping job. Soccer practice. The whole deal.

Then she provided badass backup when a rogue witch tried to take me out. That's when I found out she was a witch as well. But right now? She was acting like someone had stolen more than her ritual knife.

Carol was acting as if someone had taken a piece of her soul.

"Carol." I leaned across the table and held out a hand. She ignored it, staring through the gap in the hedge, toward the ocean and the westering sun. "How did you consecrate your blade?"

That was a personal question, and information that usually only passed from teacher to student. It wasn't something you talked about casually. And not in front of non-witches. But here we were.

She turned her head my way, eyes haunted.

"I fed it my breath, and some of my energy…"

"And?"

Her mouth opened and closed like a fish's. She whispered something, but a seagull cried at the same time, and the words left on the ocean breeze.

"I couldn't hear you. Carol. You have to tell us, or we can't help you."

But she sunk back into herself, dropping the carrot onto the patchy grass.

I took a gulp of wine and looked at Tracy and Tabitha. The two teens looked spooked, and I didn't blame them. Toby was rocking slightly, side to side, in their chair, with Cecilia's hand stroking their back, trying to soothe whatever it was away.

Stefon and Cecilia were the only two people around the table that seemed okay.

"Has she been like this a lot lately?" I asked the teens.

"Off and on," Tracy said. "Right, Tabitha?"

Tabitha nodded quickly, her knife-straight black bob bouncing at an angle around her shoulders. "For at least a couple of weeks. We finally got her to tell us her athame was missing, but that's all."

"So, we came and got you," Tracy finished.

I dug a baby carrot into the smooth surface of the hummus and crunched away. I needed time to think, and might as well get something in my stomach while I was at it. Then I remembered something.

"Cecilia? You said you had something you needed to talk to us about, too. What was it?"

My best friend patted Toby's shoulder and turned back to the rest of us.

"You know my shop boss, Raul?"

I nodded, then grabbed a couple more carrots and some more cheese, heaping them into a small pile on a napkin.

"Well, he said some of his tools were missing, but there wasn't any sign of a break-in. He thought one of the mechanics had just borrowed them and put them back in the wrong place...."

"But?" Stefon asked.

"But everyone denies doing it. I mean, we all know better than to use someone else's tools without permission! Everyone has their own locked, rolling toolbox, and usually we only share the bigger shop tools, you know?"

My hulk of a boyfriend crossed a foot over one knee.

"When did he notice the tools were missing?" he asked. Always one to get to the point.

"He told me the date, and I double checked it," Cecilia said. "He noticed they were gone the morning after the full moon."

I groaned.

"Cyrus!" I muttered to the salty air. "You can show up and offer your two cents any time now."

No answer. I stifled a sigh. I was a grown witch and

Cyrus was a busy warlock with more important things to attend to, I was sure.

It was up to me, and my ragtag group of friends, as usual. But hey, backup is backup, right?

"Carol." I reached for her hand, but she clutched them to her belly as if she was protecting herself. "You have to give us more information than that, or we can't help you."

"I know I do," she said, eyes looking haunted. "But it's as if..."

"As if what?" Tracy said. Her eyes looked sad. "Mom?"

Carol looked around the table as if noticing the rest of us were there for the first time. It was weird. Creepy even. Something was very off about this whole situation. It set my teeth on edge. The hairs on the back of my neck stood at attention, as if a ghost had just walked by. I didn't like it. Not one bit.

Stefon grabbed my hand, but I couldn't take in the comfort of it.

"Hey," he said, voice gentle. "Carol. It's okay. We got you."

Her whole body shuddered, but she nodded and licked her lips.

"Thank you," she said. "Can I have some lemonade?"

Tabitha quickly reached forward and poured her a glass, which Carol drank halfway down in one gulp.

"Ever since that ritual...and it was a good one. Powerful. I felt as if the magic was really going to do its work, you know, turn some things around in our lives, help not only me and Tracy..." She looked at the teens.

"And you too, Tabitha. But not only us. It felt like it had to power to turn around the luck of this whole town. It was big magic, you know? Not just personal magic."

"And sometimes, magic like that attracts outside attention," I muttered, half to myself.

"What happened then?" Toby asked. The hob looked intent, interested, as if they were about to uncover the deepest, most important secret they had ever heard.

"Like I said," Carol continued. "I did the ritual, cleaned up, then I just went to bed. And then the next day I woke up feeling weird."

"Weird how?" Stefon's voice was sharp now.

"Kind of hungover. It happens sometimes with intense magic, but this felt more like I'd been drinking alcohol. But I just don't drink that much, and hadn't touched any alcohol at all that night. I never do on nights when I'm doing magic."

I nodded. That was pretty common. A lot of magic workers wanted as clear a mind as possible, so the work didn't get muddied.

"But I had to go to work, you know, so I just got out of bed. Made sure Tracy was heading to the store. And that was that." She shook her head, blond hair moving softly around the drawn features of her face. "But I just didn't feel like myself. I kept making small mistakes all day. I had to redo one whole set of calculations because a customer called me on it. That was embarrassing."

I dipped a carrot into some hummus and chewed, thinking. I *really* wanted Uncle Cyrus here. Damn that warlock, anyway. Where was he?

"And then I got home," Carol continued, "after

picking Tracy up at the bookshop. We made dinner. We watched some TV."

I couldn't take the slow unfolding of this story anymore. "You're killing me, Carol. When did you notice your athame was gone?"

She looked at me, eyes sad and haunted. "Before I went to bed. I always meditate in the morning and pray at night. When I went to light a candle to say my evening prayers, my blade was gone."

4

The auto body shop Cecilia worked at was a hive of activity, which was fascinating.

I'd only ever come by to visit during slow times and had never seen it this way. Feet sticking out from beneath classic cars. Guns N' Roses blaring from hidden speakers. Wrenches clanking. The scent of grease and oil. Mechanics huddled around engines, conferring. Phones ringing. People waiting to pick up their cars. It was almost overwhelming, and I quickly threw up an extra layer around my usual psychic shields just to muffle the onslaught a bit.

I exhaled and relaxed my shoulders, which had begun to creep up around my ears.

Considering that Raul's shop specialty was classic cars, I didn't expect that rental-car-driving tourists would be a target market.

And, sure enough, all the cars in the shop were of the old, mostly shiny, variety. How in the world was this shop filled with classic cars during tourist season in a sleepy seaside town?

Cecilia jogged over in her blue coveralls, fuchsia hair tucked beneath a greasy backwards ball cap, wiping her hands on a red shop rag. Unlike me, Cecilia is a wizard with all things mechanical.

"Are you always this busy?" I asked. "I wouldn't have come by if I'd known."

"Classic car rally ten minutes up the coast. Anything goes wrong? They know to bring their cars to Raul."

"Does he have time to see me?"

Cecilia shrugged. "Not really, but things aren't going to get any slower for the next few days, and I know you need to open the bookshop."

That was the truth. Duncan was working today, so I had a little leeway, but during summers? Life for a shop owner in Seashell Cove tended to be all hands on deck.

"Come on," Cecilia said, walking across the stained concrete floor. She headed toward a baby-blue classic fin car with a Chevrolet emblem. I'm sure the car itself had some name I should know, but, what can I say? Cecilia is the gearhead and I'm a bookworm and ever has it been, and ever shall it remain.

Not that there isn't crossover. Her boss, Raul—someone who taught shop in our high school a decade ago—came into The Widening Gyre all the time. He loved thrillers and historical novels.

I spotted him gesturing at something beneath the raised hood of the blue car. He was a wiry, muscular man, with short dark hair sparkling with silvery strands along the temples. I could see the crescent scar above his right eyebrow, marring his golden-brown skin. He'd gotten the scar in a mechanical accident years ago.

Or so he always said.

"Hey Raul, got a few minutes?" Cecilia asked.

He looked up with a scowl, face clearing when he caught sight of me.

Well, at least that was a nice response. Witches didn't always get that when they showed up at your place of business.

"Sarah," he said. "Thank goodness you're here. Back in a few, folks. Figure this out while I'm gone, okay?"

That got him a bark of laughter.

"Office," Raul said, jerking his head. Cecilia and I followed him into a small room with one window facing outside and two windows facing the shop floor. A battered metal desk was piled with stacks of papers and catalogs, and three equally battered chairs were set near it, one behind, and two facing.

I had a feeling Raul spent as little time in this office as possible.

I also bet his rolling toolbox was as neat and orderly as this space was a mess.

"Can you tell me what happened?" I shifted in my chair, trying to avoid what felt like a very large spring digging into my left butt cheek.

Raul swiveled in his chair, which gave off alarming creaks and groans at every turn.

"I opened the shop as usual, switched on the lights, walked the floor, checking on the various jobs, you know? Everything seemed fine, so I headed to the break room to get coffee started."

He gazed out onto the shop floor, remembering.

"Then Tommy comes in, weird look on his face, and says, 'You gotta come see this, boss.'"

Raul paused again. Swivel. Squeak. Groan. What was it about this case that made getting people to tell me what was happening seem like I was pulling teeth?

"Boss!" Cecilia finally said, voice sharp.

He snapped out of it. Shook himself. Looked back at me.

"I checked the cars before doing the coffee thing, right? Just to see where things were. How far along. But I hadn't checked the toolboxes, because why would I? They're all locked up inside a locked garage."

"But?" I said. Because there was a *but* bigger than my ample one, hanging in the air.

Which is a really weird vision, now that I think of it. So never mind that.

"But his toolbox was unlocked," Cecilia finally filled in. "And the lid was open."

"That seems...bad," I said. Cecilia looked at me as if I'd just made the understatement of the year.

"You know how much our tools cost? Do you have any idea how much money and time we invest in building up just the right..."

"Okay, okay, Cecilia, I think Sarah gets it."

Cecilia glared at me, but shut up.

Raul sighed and mopped his brow with an old blue bandana.

"What was missing?" I asked. Raul seemed uncomfortable talking about all of this, so I stared at a Firefighters of Seashell Cove calendar on the wall. Huh. There'd always been rumors in high school that Raul was gay, but I'd never seen him around town with anyone. My guess is that being a gay mechanic in a small seaside town wasn't the easiest thing. Unless that town was Fire Island, or maybe Rehobeth. And neither of those was on the Oregon Coast.

The Oregon Coast isn't exactly a suntan-lotion-and-tiny-shorts place. It was hard to cruise someone wearing polar fleece.

But now I was the one getting distracted.

"Some crap was missing. Cheaper tools. Some wrenches. A few things that are pretty easy to replace..."

I looked back at his face, which looked haggard under the fluorescent light, as if he hadn't been sleeping well.

He raised exhausted-looking dark brown eyes up to my face.

"My favorite hammer is gone. It's...it was my father's. A beautiful, short-handled blacksmith's hammer, with a worn-in, heavy head. Hammer like that? One that's been held and used for decades? One that generations have sweated on, and bled on? It's irreplaceable."

His expression darkened.

"I could hurt whoever took it from me. And I really want it back."

5

———

I t was date night, and Stefon and I were freshly showered after our post-work beach jog. Jogging on the beach is one of my favorite activities—well, besides reading and smooching with my handsome sweetheart —but jogging on the beach during summer months is more like running an obstacle course, though not as fun.

But, hand linked with Stefon's, I felt content. We were heading down Main Street, dodging still more happy tourists and a tall person dressed like a combination clown-magician, making coins appear and disappear and fashioning balloon animals for delighted toddlers and their cranky parents.

The clown had a white greasepaint face, elaborate black eyebrows, red mouth, red nose, and a battered black top hat to go with his white shirt, suspenders, and black tuxedo pants. I looked down. Ordinary black sneakers with a red stripe down the side. I guess standing on a sidewalk all day in clown shoes played heck with your feet.

"Can we turn yet?" Stefon grumbled, after the third person smacked into him because they were looking at the kites, or Tetris's fake T-rex skeleton, or the ice cream shop, or anyplace other than where they were going.

"Yeah, let's cut over to Seagrass Lane. The restaurant is near there, anyway. You ever seen that clown before?"

"Nope," Stefon replied, "and I hope to never see him again."

I laughed. "I forget how much you loathe clowns.

Stefon shuddered elaborately, just to make me laugh more.

Yeah. He's my guy, and I love him.

We were heading to try out a new Thai place a couple blocks off Main, and I was looking forward to it. Woman cannot live off tamales, salads, and blueberry muffins alone.

Though I might be able to live off tea.

Seagrass Lane was much quieter. A mostly residential street with a few smaller shops tucked into bungalows behind manzanita bushes and small cactus gardens. The homes here looked a lot like mine. Craftsman-style, weathered wood and paint, and porches with disintegrating rattan furniture angled to take in the ocean sunsets.

The ocean sunsets were what my cottage lacked, which was why my parents had been able to afford it. Homes with views always cost more, even humble-looking places like these.

Stefon's small but swanky apartment, high up on one of the hills, had a knockout view. But Stefon made a lot more money as a computer programmer and consultant than I ever would running a brick-and-mortar bookshop.

I sighed.

"What's wrong, babe?" Stefon squeezed my hand.

"Oh. You know. The bookshop's doing better, but it still doesn't bring in quite enough revenue. And the teens..."

"They have some great ideas, babe. I think you should give them a chance."

"You're right. And I am. It's just..."

We walked in silence for a moment, listening to toddlers shrieking along with the seagulls, somewhere down where rocky cliffs met sand and the wild Pacific.

"I know that it's silly, but it still feels wrong to change things."

Stefon stopped walking and pulled me close. He smelled warm. Comforting. Like castile soap and home.

"If you want to keep your dad's memory alive by keeping the bookstore open..."

"Then I have to actually keep the bookstore open," I finished. "I know. Like I said, it's foolish."

He kissed my forehead. "It's not foolish, though. I get it. But I also think it's time to make some changes. The teens want to help you with that? I say let 'em."

We resumed our walk, skirting past car bumpers that poked out onto the sidewalk. Stefon picked up a dropped doll and set it gently on a low rock wall surrounding one of the homes.

"Hey," he said. "What's that?"

"What's what?"

"That store. It's new."

I followed his pointing finger, and sure enough, there was a freshly painted, small white bungalow next door. And, staked in a garden bed on a neat walkway leading up to a turquoise-blue door, was a painted sign.

Inquire Within: Tarot, Psychic Readings, and Astrology.

"Huh. That's definitely new."

And strange. As a witch and a Justice, I should have known a psychic was setting up shop in town. I mean, it wasn't illegal or anything, but the Witches and Warlocks Council—which I was now a reluctant member of, because A, they're a bunch of old fuddy duddies, and B, who has time?—tried to keep track of stuff like this.

Mostly, they kept tabs to keep innocent bystanders from being fleeced by charlatans, which happened a lot in towns like Seashell Cove. But also? If someone was a real psychic? That meant they had a sparkle of magic, at very least. And if magic was being used?

The Council should know.

"How did I not know about this?" I exhaled loudly.

"I don't know, babe. Could be that A, you've been a little busy and B, you can't know everything that's going on in this town."

"But a psychic reader?" I looked at my boyfriend, who just shrugged and ran a hand over his beard to smooth what was already perfect.

Yeah, I should have known there was a new psychic in town. Or a fortune teller. Or whatever they were. I was not only a witch. I was a Justice. And I suddenly felt like I'd been derelict in my brand new duties. That wasn't good.

I looked down the neat walkway past the Japanese maple trees at the cute Craftsman cottage. It looked harmless enough with its fresh white paint, but who knew?

"I'm going in." I said.

"Babe." Stefon planted his feet on the sidewalk and crossed his arms over his massive chest. He gave me one of his looks.

"They're closed," he said. "We're en route to dinner. I just want to have a date with my girl, not investigate whatever this is, or whatever you think this is. Is that too much to ask?"

Now it was my turn to give him a look. I crossed my own arms over my equally ample chest. Though admittedly, mine is a lot more soft tissue than muscle. I raised an eyebrow.

"Babe, not the eyebrow."

I smirked. He sighed.

"All right...guess we're knocking on the door. Let's do whatever this is."

He opened the white picket gate, and we made our way up the walk. Place definitely looked closed, which made sense for a weekday evening, even during the summer. And I wasn't getting any bad vibes off it. Oh, you might think vibes are hogwash. But they're not. Vibes are the main ways witches sense things. Other psychics, too. And empaths. You know that feeling you get when someone's standing too close to you? Vibes. You know that feeling you get when you want someone to stand even closer? That's vibes, too. The feeling that no way in heck are you walking into the abandoned building? Yeah. Vibes.

At any rate, the neat little white cottage with its turquoise door actually gave off good vibes. Huh.

"Okay, here goes," I said, knocking on the wood doorframe. We waited. Heard what sounded like the world's lightest person walking toward us. The door opened a crack and a small, delicate face under a shock of dark hedgehog hair stared up at me.

"Ash?" I said. "What are you doing here?"

This time both his eyebrows shot up toward his forehead. "Dad," he called over his shoulder, "Sarah from the bookshop is here."

I could have sworn I heard a stifled groan coming from farther back in the building, but in short order, padding towards me in a pair of slippers... Sure enough, it was Jerry Hamamoto, looking tense.

"Sarah..." he began.

"We have a lot of talking to do," I replied.

He sighed. "I suppose you're right. Do you want to come in?"

From behind me Stefon said, "Actually, we were just heading out to dinner. Can you join us?

Mr. Hamamoto paused for a moment, and ran a hand over his smooth chin. "I guess I could. Ash, you want to come?"

"I already ate, Dad. Can I stay here and read my new book?"

A kid after my own heart.

"I suppose that's all right. I should only be an hour, and we'll be..." He raised a questioning eyebrow.

"Just down the street at Thai Taste."

"Okay. Anything happens, you text me."

"All right, Dad."

Mr. Hamamoto ruffled his son's hair, then set his jaw, as if bracing for an Inquisition.

"Just let me get my shoes on. I'll be right with you."

6

———

Thai Taste was a new business that I actually knew about, unlike Jerry Hamamoto's place. Well cushioned wood booths lined the walls beneath windows that looked out on the tree-lined street half a block off Main. It was a great location, actually. Quieter than the main drag through town, yet close enough to still get good foot traffic without customers needing to search too hard. A water feature splashed near the front entrance, and broad-leafed plants dotted the tile floor, creating cozy nooks out of the tables in the center of the room.

"Peanut sauce," I groaned. "And sautéed peppers."

The place smelled so freaking good I might never leave.

Too bad I was working, and not just on a nice date with my boyfriend, like he'd asked for.

In the booth next to me, Stefon looked unbothered, perusing the menu. I could hear the subtle *tap tap tap* of Jerry's feet beneath the table across from me.

He must know he was in some kind of trouble. Which meant he knew exactly who I was when he brought Ash into my store and acted as if they were just the new kids in town, aw shucks and thank you.

I flushed with heat and huffed out a breath, distracted from the menu by the problem sitting across from me.

"Babe," Stefon said softly, placing a hand on my thigh. "What do you want to eat?"

The question was a reminder: *Don't start a fight in public. Play nice.*

For a man who bashed people's heads in for fun on the weekends, Stefon sure was diplomatic.

"Massaman curry with a side of green papaya salad."

"Want to share?"

I looked at his big frame, which, frankly, barely fit into the booth. "Share with you and whose army?"

He grinned, lighting up his face. "Point taken."

Finally, a waitperson took our order and refilled our water glasses. We thanked her, fiddled with our napkins for a moment, and then I leveled my gaze back at the slight, handsome man across the table from me. He looked to be in his mid to late thirties, with hair as dark as Ash's, but cut to fall in a soft wave over his forehead. Black-rimmed glasses perched on a narrow nose.

"Mr. Hamamoto, you haven't been entirely honest with me."

Gah. I sounded like my dad did whenever I was in trouble. When had that happened? I was only twenty-eight years old, for Pete's sake.

His Adam's apple bobbed as he drank some water,

ice clashing around in his glass. My glass sat untouched, sweating on its white paper coaster.

I bet Jerry here was sweating, too.

Finally, he set his glass down and dropped his head into his hands.

"I'm a *wrrmph*."

I looked at Stefon, who shrugged, then looked around the restaurant, probably searching for the wait-person with his beer.

"You're a what?"

Jerry's small, dark eyes raised just enough to catch mine.

"I'm a *witch*." Still whispering, he practically hissed that last word at me, as if it was a curse, rather than something natural. Something that some people trained diligently toward, and that others were simply born with.

"Why didn't you tell me? You know you're supposed to check in with at least some of the local magical beings when you move to a new place."

The waitperson took that exact moment to arrive with a giant tray filled with the most delectable-smelling food. My annoyance at the interruption was blunted by the fact that my mouth was watering.

Had I forgotten to eat lunch again?

Oh. Yeah. I had.

Stefon got his beer, and the server set down a metal teapot and two small cups.

We thanked her again, then set about enacting the sacred ritual of portioning out the food.

Fragrant rice. Rich curry. Tangy green papaya.

Yeah. Stefon was right. We should've just had our date and left whatever this business was for tomorrow.

"You're always impetuous, my little witchling." My mother's voice rang inside my head. Her memory struck me in the heart.

I missed her. Missed both of my parents. But they were gone, I was here, and much as I still questioned myself sometimes, I was the local magical Justice.

The community trusted me. So, here I was.

We ate in silence for a few minutes. Despite my impatience, I think we all needed it. Stefon put down his fork and picked up his pint glass of golden Thai beer.

"You were going to tell us about being a witch. And being here in Seashell Cove."

Jerry chewed, looking out the window.

"Ash and I were run out of our last town."

Well, knock me over with a Rachel Caine thriller.

"You were what?" I choked out. I reached for the tea and took a reassuring swallow of the fragrant, green brew.

Tea would get me through this conversation.

"Ash...he started manifesting strange powers. Things started flying through the air at school. Pens. Books. Basketballs. Art supplies. You name it, Ash was throwing it against walls."

I sat back, trying to wrap my mind around that sweet kid using telekinesis to scare their schoolmates.

"Was Ash being bullied?" Stefon asked. He kept his voice soft, but I could hear the growl beneath it.

Jerry nodded. "We lived in rural Oregon. It was where

my former partner grew up, and after he died, I thought it would be good for Ash to be close to family. My family is all in St. Louis, but we both love Oregon so much…"

"What happened?" I asked.

"A few of the kids started bullying Ash for being trans. They kept saying 'You're a girl, you freak!'"

Jerry drank some more water.

"But something else happened, didn't it?" Stefon asked. "You said you got run out of town."

I'd already forgotten that part.

"Two teachers got involved. Started treating Ash badly. Then they roped some parents into their crappy little campaign against my child." He wiped his mouth as if the white napkin could wipe away the bad taste twisting his face into a grimace. "My child. My smart, funny, beautiful child…"

"And you got mad," I said, finally catching up.

Lips pursed, he gave a sharp nod.

"Okay," I said. "We're going to get to the bottom of this story, but first? I think I want a beer."

Stefon raised his hand to flag down the waiter.

"Good idea," Jerry said. "I don't usually drink on school nights, but I'll make an exception this time."

Pint glasses of crisp lager procured and food packed into go cartons, I straightened my spine and got back to the conversation at hand.

"I really like your kid, Jerry. It's okay that I call you Jerry, right?"

"Of course."

"I really like your kid, and I want to like you, but right now? I don't trust you."

Stefon shifted in the booth, thigh bumping mine, but he didn't say anything.

"That's fair enough," Jerry replied. "I probably wouldn't trust me, either."

"So, tell us what happened. As much as you can."

I took a sip of beer, mostly to keep from staring holes into Jerry's head. It was good. Crisp. I could see why Stefon liked it.

"I wanted to go in, guns blazing, you know?"

"But you didn't," Stefon said.

"But I didn't. I bided my time. Gathered supplies. Waited for the next full moon."

I continued to sip. Waiting. This story was shaping up to be something good.

Or very bad. Depended how you looked at it.

"The full moon coincided with the school play."

Stefon groaned, but just took another swallow of beer.

"I rigged a trap for the two teachers and the parents who were in on the campaign against Ash. I made sure Ash stayed home. Convinced Ash he wasn't feeling well."

I hissed. Coercion is a pretty serious crime.

He flapped a hand. "I know. I know. But I needed to keep him safe, you know? It's all I ever wanted. To keep my son safe."

"We get it, man," Stefon said. "But we need to know the rest."

"I wanted something that would affect those teachers and parents, make them feel as bad as they'd made Ash feel. But I was careful to not really hurt them, you know?"

"But someone got hurt anyway," I said. They always did.

He nodded again. "Mrs. Roberts. When my remorse spell hit, she stumbled into the path of a car pulling into the lot. They were going faster than they should have been. A parent, late, who thought everyone would be inside."

"Did she die?" Stefon asked. How his voice remained that calm, I didn't know. I was practically sitting on the edge of my seat, and no amount of beer or tea was going to calm me down.

"She broke her arm. But they all knew. They knew it was me."

He sighed, finished off his beer with three long, desperate swallows, and smacked the empty pint glass down.

"Ash was suspended and people started boycotting my business. Picketing. Shouting. Throwing red paint on the door."

"So you left," I said.

"So we left." He finally looked me in the eye. There was a slight hint of defiance there, which was a good thing. It meant that Jerry Hamamoto hadn't given up.

"We came here to start over, and I hope you can see why I wasn't exactly keen to rush in and announce that I was the new witch in town."

I got that. In his shoes? I probably would have done the same.

But it wasn't lost on me that a new witch had arrived in secret, with a telekinetic son, and people's tools had started to disappear.

7

———

S tefon and I stayed up talking late into the night.

I still didn't know what to think about Jerry Hamamoto, the missing tools, or any of the rest of it. Knowing that Duncan was on open-the-bookshop duty, I gave myself a slow start.

After a walk on the beach and a quick stop at Angie's Blueberry Café, I was finally heading back up Main Street toward The Widening Gyre. It always lifted my heart to walk toward the bookshop. To see the bright window displays of some of my favorite books enticing readers in off the street. I was so relieved the bookstore was doing slightly better these days.

Whether it was that we were out of the winter doldrums and well into summer, or whether it was the energy the teens brought to the shop... The teens and all their ideas, I should say. Ideas that I resisted at first. They were softening me up.

I smiled at Rhiannon glaring at me through the window. The cat definitely had an attitude. Taking a deep breath of blueberry muffin–scented air, I shifted the sack of baked goods and opened the door to the clattering of bells and the sound of bluegrass music coming over the speakers. Duncan had eclectic taste.

I could hear him in the science fiction aisle, helping a customer. Tracy and Tabitha huddled around the computer at the front desk, conferring intently.

"You're here!" Tabitha said. "We have so much to show you."

Whereas once I would have stifled a groan, today the sight of them was the bomb. I smiled.

"I brought baked goods. Why don't you go put the kettle on, and you can tell me all about it."

No matter what was going on in the world, tea and books would make it right. Or at least, in my immediate part of the world. I couldn't do much about global issues, but I could do my best to take care of my little patch. My friends and my community. Much as I sometimes fretted over the larger stuff, it was tea, muffins, work, and magic that brought me back home. And that would have to be enough for now.

I greeted Duncan's customers, a couple of women around my age. Tourists, from the look of their going-to-get-cold-later clothing. Maybe I should talk to the teens about adding sweatshirts to the T-shirt order. Despite it being the Oregon Coast, there were still enough tourists who assumed "seaside" meant "hot" to make a quick sale of something that wasn't shorts.

As Duncan rang them up, I idly flipped through the mail, wondering where the heck Uncle Cyrus was. I was starting to worry. Usually he came pretty quickly when I called. Either he was busy on another case, or he thought this was something I should handle on my own. I shrugged.

Duncan's customers headed toward the door.

"Thank you for coming in." I waved. "Hope you enjoy your books."

"Oh, we will," said one of the women. The other smiled and held up her stack of books like trophies. I laughed.

"Hey Duncan, how are things going? I've got baked goods."

"So I smell," he said. This week, Duncan's hair was bleached blond and his heavy black-rimmed glasses stood out against his pale skin in stark contrast. He wore an ancient Dead Kennedys T-shirt. I had no idea where he even got the stuff. But along with bluegrass, nineties hip hop, and folk metal, he loved old school punk, through and through.

"I'm gonna take these to the back. What flavor should I save you? I got a chocolate chip if you want one."

"Aces." He gave me two thumbs up and then headed back to restocking shelves. I found both teens bustling around the tiny pocket kitchen next to the restroom. They were chattering excitedly about something, as I pushed open the door.

The scent of boiling water hitting my favorite English breakfast tea blended with the delectable smell of the baked goods I still carried. Tabitha was pouring the water into the big Brown Betty teapot as Tracy got down mugs and poured creamer into my grandmother's old jug.

"Hey there," I said. "What has you two all excited?"

Tabitha smiled like the cat that had the cream and placed the Brown Betty lid on with a clink. Tracy practically bounced in her sneakers.

"We're getting a lot of traction on the social media accounts," Tracy said. "The shop's Instaphoto account is blowing up."

They shared a conspiratorial smile.

"And?" I asked.

"Weeelll…" Tabitha drew the word out.

"Tell me what's going on."

"Everyone's really excited about Biff!" Tracy blurted.

I knew this was coming, but that didn't mean it still didn't make me squirm.

"What do you mean?"

"Well, we started posting the books he throws around. As, you know, evidence." Tracy said, bouncing in her sneakers.

"Evidence," I said.

"Yeah, you know, like, evidence of the supernatural. That a ghost can actually pick things up and throw them." Tabitha explained in an *I'm being very clear and patient right now* voice.

Speaking of throwing the whole conversation reminded me of Ash.

"What do you two know about poltergeists?"

"Well, there's that freaky old movie, my mom loves," Tracy said. "Walk to the light, Carol Aaaaannnnn," she said in her creepiest old psychic lady voice.

I smirked. "Not the movie." Though I liked the movie too, I had to admit. My parents and I had watched it a bazillion times.

"Oh, you mean real poltergeists," Tabitha said.

"When we were studying about ghosts, trying to find out more about how to communicate with Biff, we came across a lot of information on them."

She picked up the laden tray and looked at me. "You do realize that poltergeists aren't ghosts, right?"

I will not roll my eyes. I will not roll my eyes. I will not roll my eyes.

"Yes, of course," I said. "I know they're usually kids around the cusp of adolescence, right?"

"Right," Tabitha said. "Well, if you know about them, why are you asking us?" She wrinkled her nose and raised the tray an inch. "And are we taking this out?"

"Yeah," I said, "to the reading nook."

I followed the teens through the bookshop to my favorite spot with two comfy armchairs reupholstered in striped, burgundy fabric. A low table sat beneath the stained-glass window. The summer sun picked out the bright spines of a stack of books with a black cat set on top. The stained-glass image made me wonder if Biff had had a cat like Rhiannon. I'd have to look more carefully through the pictures on the walls. There was also a box of old photos in the back storeroom. Maybe I'd set the teens to looking through those, too. But I was getting distracted now.

"I'm just wondering what besides the onset of puberty causes poltergeists," I said. "I mean, not everyone ends up manifesting that way. So, what's the key? But before we get started on all that, Tracy, would you bring a chocolate chip muffin and a cup of tea up to Duncan?"

"Sure thing. Don't say any more till I get back."

I flopped down as Tabitha grabbed another comfy chair and dragged it over. It was seriously great having responsible teenagers around.

I took a bite of blueberry muffin, and then poured some milk into a blue ceramic mug. When I added the tea, the fragrance swirled up around my head as the brown tea mixed with the white of the milk.

Tracy was back in short order. She snagged a muffin and plopped into the extra chair Tabitha had dragged over. "We found out a bunch of stuff about poltergeists. It mostly manifests in kids at their teens who have latent psychic skills and have been…"

She looked at Tabitha, who finished the sentence. "Who were under some kind of pressure."

"Pressure?" I asked.

"You know…" Tracy swallowed her muffin bite and picked up the thread again. "Could be pressure to excel, pushed too hard by parents or guardians…"

"Or being bullied," Tabitha added.

Right. That would explain it.

We sipped our tea and ate our muffins for a while.

"Why are you asking all these questions about poltergeists?" Tabitha asked.

I set my mug down on the small table. "There's a new kid in town. A trans kid named Ash, and his dad is worried about him. I guess he got bullied at his last school."

"That sucks," Tabitha said, picking at her muffin crumbs.

"Yeah," Tracy agreed.

"Yeah," I said, raising my eyebrows. "It does suck."

"We need to help him," Tracy said.

I was coming to that conclusion myself, but first I had to figure out what was happening with Ash's father. Something still didn't sit right about the whole situation, much as I liked them both at first glance. There were still too many unanswered questions.

"Okay," I said, "enough about that."

I patted my the crumbs off my hands, picked up my mug, and settled back into my chair.

"Let's talk about the missing tools. And Carol. We need to get on this."

8

I left the teens to do some research and gave them a go-ahead to order two new T-shirt designs and yes, to play up the fact that the bookshop had a resident ghost.

I still felt a bit queasy about all that. As an introvert, anything that shone a public spotlight anywhere near me made me squirm. Bad enough that as a Justice, magical beings were looking at me more and more.

Despite all of that, I had to admit that their efforts so far had brought in enough business that I could pay their part-time salaries and give Duncan a raise. Heck, if this growth spurt continued, I could even pay some more of my expenses, and any small business owner will tell you that paying yourself is usually the thing that comes last. So yeah, the teens were doing well. Duncan seemed happy. Heck, even Rhiannon was in a better mood lately.

I wondered what was up with that. Maybe I would

spring for a new bed for her, though knowing her, she would just forsake a fancy cat bed for a pile of books.

Me? I could use some time in my own bed with a pile of books. But that wish was for the winter doldrums, not for the height of summer, and not when there was a possible thief ransacking Seashell Cove. It was time for me to hit the pavement and start asking some questions.

First stop was Ancient Treasures, with its T-Rex flag flapping in the wind and the flat-pack dinosaur skeletons taking pride of place on the wide sidewalk out front. Tetris always had clever displays. And as long as he was careful to not block the sidewalk, the Seashell Cove City Council was fine with it. Anything to keep the tourists happy and spending cash.

Tetris and I traded customers back and forth. He carried a small selection of specialty books on fossil hunting in the area, plus the usual dino books for kids. Anything he didn't have? He sent them down my way. I did the same for him.

I pushed open the glass door, and was greeted by the roar of a T-Rex. Scared me every time. Tetris was behind the counter, showing off some fossils to a couple of teenagers. Two boys in Keds, baggy pants, and T-shirts.

An aging punk rocker in burgundy Doc Martens, a Dead Kennedys T-shirt, and faded gray jeans that matched his gray hair, Tetris was good with young people.

With Tracy and Tabitha around, I was getting better with young people. At least I hoped so. He gave me a nod and held up a give-me-a-minute finger. Browsing for a few spare minutes was fine with me. I loved looking around his store, and headed past the fossils to a small display of bones and was soon in deep examination of a marmot skull. So cool.

"What's up, Sarah?" he said, startling me.

"Where do you get this stuff?" I asked, and not for the first time. He laughed.

"Oh, you know, around. What brings you by today?"

I looked around. The teens were still engrossed in the display case by the cash point. Two white kids, one tall and a little chunky, and the other shorter. Younger. Over his T-shit, the tall one wore a jean jacket with ripped-off sleeves and the Donnie Darko rabbit on a back patch. With their sandy brown hair and tanned faces, they looked related.

A couple of toddlers sat on the floor next to the picture books, with two adults nearby, keeping a not-very-careful watch. No one was close enough to listen in, unless they had some spooky preternatural hearing ability. And so far I hadn't heard of any magic workers in the area who had that particular skill set.

I lowered my voice anyway. "Have you noticed if anything's gone missing from the store recently?" I asked. Might as well dive right in. Tetris knew me well enough to see through any prevarication anyway. We always tried to be pretty direct with each other.

He rubbed his jaw. "You know, I thought it was just a mistake I'd made in counting inventory. But now that you mentioned it, a fossil blade went missing. And some jet beads and an amber pendant."

"Fossil blade?" I asked.

"I'll show you," he said, and walked down a few feet

to another display case. Sure enough, there were fossils. Some black earthy substance filled with what looked like little trilobites formed into points. It was a nice shape that I bet fit well in the palm of your hand.

"You think one of these is missing?"

"Yeah," he said, "maybe two by my count."

"Are they particularly valuable?"

"Not in the larger scheme of things. I mean, they're not particularly rare fossils or anything, but still, it's inventory."

I nodded, staring down at the shining lumps of ancient stone. Neither of us needed to say more than that. Small, independent shops like ours couldn't afford to lose much. We operated on that narrow of a margin, unlike large chain stores owned by billionaire conglomerates.

"See you around, Tetris!" the Donnie Darko teen called as they left the shop, T-Rex roaring.

Tetris waved.

"They local?" I asked.

"Just moved here from Sacramento," he replied. "Their mom got a job with that local publisher, I think."

Huh. Not that people didn't move to Seashell Cove. It happened. But not often. So two families with teens in one summer? Seemed a bit unusual to me.

I also wondered why I hadn't seen those two in the shop yet. *Not everyone's a reader, Sarah.*

I dragged my attention back to Tetris, who was busy making slight adjustments to the fossil display, filling in gaps.

"How about the amber pendant? Valuable?"

Again, he shrugged. "It wasn't the most expensive one I have. Why are you asking? I take it other things are missing?"

One of the toddlers shrieked happily. The adults murmured.

I looked around the store, and out the windows at Main Street, shining in the sun. Why had I ever thought Seashell Cove was a sleepy town?

"Yeah, it's looking that way. If you hear anything, will you let me know?"

"Of course."

I patted his arm and turned to go.

"Hey, you and Stefon interested in going bowling sometime?" he called out. I paused before exiting the door and smiled.

"You know what? That sounds like fun. Send me a text."

It was good he wanted to get out again. Do things. After his girlfriend was killed by a very remorseful ghost and a would-be reporter, Tetris had gone all hermity for a while. I couldn't blame him.

"Will do," he said, "and keep me posted."

I wave a hand in acknowledgment, then shoved out the door, dodging a heavily laden stroller and a corgi.

The T-Rex roared.

$$9$$

My next stop was the Blueberry Café. Sure, I wanted to talk to Angie, who saw almost everything that went on in town, but I was also getting hungry for lunch.

I skirted the clown, who bowed and offered me a pink carnation with a message ribbon tied around the stem.

"Thank you, clown!" I stopped to hunt for a dollar to throw in the black leather case sitting open on the ground. The clown had already turned away, spying three children heading his way.

I shrugged. Didn't have a dollar on me, anyway. I glanced down at the ribbon. *Your luck may change today,* it read. Huh.

Hope that meant something good.

I was walking past Bart's pottery shop, which is my favorite place to buy tea mugs, and was just about to cross the street to Angie's, but I had to wait for a stream of cars to go by. Of course. Summer traffic is a you-know-what.

Behind me, I heard a "*Psssst!* Sarah!"

I turned, and there was Bart himself. He was as stocky as Tetris was gangly. A short, nervous-looking white guy with sandy hair and bright blue eyes, Bart was a total sweetheart, and had the world's most talented hands. I swear, the man could take a lump of clay and make the most beautiful things in the world.

I stepped away from the crosswalk. "Hey Bart."

He looked around, as if making sure none of the tourists were listening in.

"Do you need something?" I asked.

He glanced back into his shop, which was filled with shoppers.

"Can you talk after work tonight? It's important."

I peered into those blue eyes, and underneath his usual nervous expression, I saw a flash of worry. Well, wasn't that interesting. I glanced at my watch.

"Sure. I can come by after closing. You'll be here?"

He nodded.

"Thanks," he said, and scurried back inside.

Well, that was strange. Since I'd become Justice, things in Seashell Cove sure seemed fraught. Was it me, or was this just the way things had always been, and my parents and uncle had protected me from it? I shrugged, looked both ways, and ran across Main Street to the Blueberry Café, a conference with Angie, and hopefully an early lunch.

The warm smells of cinnamon, sugar, and coffee assaulted me as soon as I opened the door. I hurried past the community notice board with its layers of flyers and posters flapping, and headed to the counter.

Thankfully, there wasn't a line. I had timed it properly so I'd hit the café between the morning and lunchtime rushes. It's the little things that make life good, right?

"Hey Sarah," Angie greeted me from behind the counter, her hair pulled back under her usual blueberry-blue kerchief and her blueberry-blue apron tied over regulation jeans and T-shirt. "What can I get you?"

She was a curvy, attractive woman, and I used to wonder why she wasn't dating. I'd finally figured out she probably wasn't interested. The teens had been teaching me about asexuality, and helped me figure out some people are just wired that way. Kind of like I'm wired bisexual.

I had the menu memorized, but perused the board anyway, just for fun.

"A tuna melt on your house-baked rye, and an English Breakfast tea, please."

"Coming right up!" She rang me up, pressed the button that sent the order back to the kitchen, and turned back to me with a smile.

"Do you have a few minutes?" I said.

"Sure. I need to sit down before the lunch rush hits anyway. Just let me grab a coffee and your tea. I'll find you."

She waved me off toward the blond wood tables that dotted the café floor. I avoided the big, Main Street–facing windows. Didn't really want anyone watching this conversation, because I wasn't sure what would come up.

I forsook the bright open spaces and sunshine and headed to the back of the café, where a few tables sat tucked near a corner bookcase and a scattering of comfy chairs for folks who wanted to just sip their coffee and read awhile. Did I mention how much I like Angie's café?

Angie set our mugs down with a thunk, and slid into a chair across the table from me.

"What's up with the carnation? Stefon feeling romantic?"

I stirred some creamer into my tea, watching the milky liquid suffuse into the deep, rich brown. I looked at my friend's round, expectant face.

"No. That clown across the street handed it to me."

"That's nice." She sipped her coffee. "What did you want to talk about?"

"Have you noticed anything strange lately?"

Angie practically snorted out her coffee. "Strange in Seashell Cove? You'll have to be a little more specific than that."

Angie wasn't a witch, and had no magic other than what she put into her baked goods—which takes considerable talent, I must say—but she'd seen enough of our town's magical underbelly over the years. It rightfully made her suspicious of anything that looked out of the ordinary. Plus, like I said, Angie saw a lot here at work. People never think wait staff or sales clerks are watching what they do. But trust me. We are.

"Things missing," I said. "Have you noticed or heard anything?"

She sat back in her chair and tapped a finger against her blueberry-festooned mug. "Well, now that you mention it. Some of our plates have gone missing."

"Your plates."

Now that was strange. Who in the world would

steal plates from the local café? They were just ordinary round white plates with a cluster of blueberries on the rim, matching the mugs. I mean they were nice and all, but... Angie looked just as baffled as I felt.

"I know, right?" she said. "But three plates are missing."

"How do you even know?" I asked.

"Clarita told me." She motioned to the server who was bringing over my sandwich. A dark-skinned Latine woman with hips as round as mine and a smile as big as the sun.

"Right, Clarita?"

"Right about what?" she asked, setting down my sandwich. It smelled divine.

"Some of our dishes went missing," Angie repeated.

"Oh yeah," Clarita said, wiping her hands on her own blueberry-blue apron. "It was weird. There were three different tables where people had eaten lunch. I'd gotten a little bit behind because of the rush, and when I went to clear those tables, the mugs and utensils were there..."

She looked out toward the front windows as if thinking, remembering. "But the plates were gone."

"And you're sure they had plates before?" I asked.

She looked at me as if I were a fool, telling her she didn't know how to do her job. I raised my hands.

"Sorry. No offense, but it just seems strange to me."

She leveled her dark eyes at me. "That's because it is strange. Something's going on in this town lately, and I don't know what. But it doesn't feel right. Things have been off all summer."

With that, she turned away and headed back to the kitchen. I looked at Angie, who just shook her head.

"She's been agitated ever since it happened. And," she said, "I tried to write it off as nothing. You know, tourists are weird. They like the strangest things as souvenirs."

"But don't you sell your plates?" I asked. Then I took a bite of my tuna melt. The rye was toasted to perfection. The cheese was melted just so... Yum.

Angie nodded, ignoring my love affair with my sandwich. "Plates, T-shirts, mugs, aprons...you name it, we sell it. But some people either don't want to pay, or they like the thrill of getting away with something. At any rate, is that all you need to know? I have to get back to work." She pushed back her chair and picked her coffee cup.

"Thanks Angie," I said, "I'll talk to you later."

She paused. "You keep me updated, you hear?" Her voice was fierce.

"I'll do that," I said, then looked down at my delicious sandwich. It still smelled amazing, but I was suddenly not so hungry anymore.

10

———

S tefon and I sat at my little two top kitchen table, eating giant salads with fresh, seared tuna on top. Stefon smelled like peppermint soap and the tangy beer he was drinking. I stuck with seltzer water. I needed to keep my wits about me.

I didn't want to, though. All I wanted was to curl up with my boyfriend, maybe watch a movie, smooch a bit. Then go to sleep.

But I had a case to crack.

"I just don't understand it," I said. "The things that have been stolen or gone missing make no sense."

Stefon had a piece of paper and a pen at his side. "Tell me what they were again?"

"Three blueberry plates, a blacksmith's hammer—which is a family heirloom—a fossil knife, some jet beads and maybe an amber pendant, Carol's athame, and a ceramic goblet."

"Ceramic. Goblet." Stephon wrote.

That last was Bart's. I had stopped by his place after work, but didn't get much information from him.

"Bart said he came in the morning before he saw me and the back door to the shop was unlocked, and his newest goblet was missing."

Stefon tapped his pen on the table.

"Look, I may not practice magic myself, but I certainly hang out with a bunch of witches—and enough Wiccans in the Society, too—to know that these all sound like elemental tools to me."

"Of course they are."

"But you're right, it still doesn't make any sense. Why?" he asked, stabbing his tuna and shoving a fork full of salad in his mouth. I followed suit. We both chewed for a while. Thinking.

"Okay. First of all," Stefon said, "why three plates? Why not one? Second of all, these weren't all already magical tools. So what's up with that?"

"Third of all," said a voice from the living room, "you're not looking at this from the right direction."

"Holy kamoly, Uncle Cyrus!" I shouted. "What have I told you about popping in with no warning?"

And sure enough, standing in the doorway to the kitchen, looking dapper as always, dark, shaved head gleaming in the kitchen lights, was my Uncle Cyrus. Oh, we aren't related by blood, but he'd been my mother's best friend and confidant and was sort of a Goddess parent to me. He's a warlock, not a witch, and that has nothing to do with gender, by the way. All that means is that Cyrus has slightly different skills and talents than I do. He was part of the Super Secret Spooky Witches and Warlocks Council. In my mind, he should have replaced my dad as Justice in town. Not me.

But he didn't want to get stuck in Seashell Cove. Cyrus had too many other important things to do, he always said. Speaking of which...

"Where have you been? I asked, setting down my fork. "I've been calling you."

"I've been busy," he said, "attending to some of the same things you are here. Unfortunately, it seems our cases are converging."

"Missing tools?" Stefon asked, then took a sip of his beer.

Uncle Cyrus snooped around the kitchen. "I don't suppose you have an open bottle of decent wine?"

"No." I snapped. Well, I did. I had a perfectly serviceable pinot grigio in the fridge, but I wasn't about to let him know that.

"Water, then?" he asked.

"Grab a glass and take a seat," I said, gesturing to the bottle of seltzer water on the table. "Have at it."

Cyrus furrowed his brow at me. What can I say? I know I wasn't usually this rude, but I was severely annoyed with him for ignoring my psychic calls.

"What case are you working on, man?" Stefon asked.

Traitor. I glared at both men. Call me childish, but I wasn't ready to cut Uncle Cyrus slack just yet. Sure, I was being petty. But that's what families are for, right?

"You know the old Fuller Mansion in Portland?" Uncle Cyrus asked once he had poured his bubbly water.

"Sure," Stefon said. "That place is dope. I love going

there around Yule time. The Pittock Mansion, too. My friends and I dig the decorations, but mostly, I love the old architecture."

I looked at him, surprised. "How come you've never taken me there?"

"I was gonna ask you this coming season," he said. "Besides, I never knew you were interested."

I shrugged and stabbed my salad as if it had wronged me. I mean, Stefon was right. Why would he know? And I wasn't surprised he'd been to the mansion, once I thought about it. Stefon was interested in anything that had to do with history, including the old timber baron mansions on the edge of our closest city.

"You're in a rather pissy mood," Uncle Cyrus said.

"Yeah, well, I have a lot on my mind," I said.

Cyrus shrugged, rolled up the sleeves of his crisp white button down shirt, and took a sip of water.

But even I had to admit that didn't explain it. I guess he decided to ignore me, which is just as well. I was annoyed with him, but couldn't exactly pinpoint why. Something else was off. And it had my hackles up.

"Getting back to what I was saying..." Uncle Cyrus said.

My thoughts rolled on. It wasn't just that he hadn't come when I called, I mean, I knew he was busy and all, but he'd been my mentor for a long time, and I was used to his help.

"...missing."

"Wait, what?" I had missed something important, that was clear.

"Babe," Stefon said, "you have to pay attention."

"I'm sorry, what did you say?" I turned to Uncle Cyrus, who was tracing patterns in the condensation on the edge of his glass.

"Elias Fuller was a Mason," he said, "and some of his regalia is missing, and the mansion ghosts are in an uproar."

"That's where you've been?" I asked.

He nodded, a grave look on his face.

"What did they take?" I asked, "A staff, a sword, a book? His apron?"

"Apron?" Stefon asked.

I waved a hand, "Aprons are very important to Freemasons, as part of their, you know, garb." I was trying to use language Stefon would understand, and garb was something he knew as well as coding or D&D.

Cyrus cleared his throat.

"His Masonic ring with a ruby in the center. It's gone."

Stefon whistled.

"Holy Mother," I said. "That seems really bad."

Uncle Cyrus nodded. "It is. It's very, very bad. It's almost as bad as when that fool stole John Dee's mirror. Oh, not quite as dangerous. But still, a thirtieth-degree Mason's ring? That's some serious business."

"Who could possibly be doing all this?" Stefon asked.

"And why such a strange variety of tools from so many different places?" I chimed in. "And what about the ghosts?" My mouth was suddenly dry as the implication set in. I gulped my water and shoved my salad to the side.

"I was hoping you might have some leads," Uncle Cyrus said. I shook my head.

"The only possible lead is the new witch in town."

Uncle Cyrus's expression didn't change.

Wait a minute.

"You knew about him, didn't you?" I said.

He shrugged. "Jerry Hamamoto is harmless. A good psychic, though, he actually knows his stuff and has real talent."

"How can you know that he's harmless?" I sputtered. "He came to town, and all of a sudden things start going missing. Not all of the magical tools, granted. But still...and his son is a poltergeist."

"A what?" Stefon asked, almost spitting out his beer. "Dang. You can't just spring that on a person, Sarah."

"Oh, yeah. I didn't mention that, did I?"

"I thought poltergeists were ghosts." Stefon said, stabbing at his salad. Uncle Cyrus and I both gave him a look.

"Movies aside, you should know better than that," Uncle Cyrus replied. His voice was mild, but I could tell he was amused. "Poltergeists are actually just telekinetic teens."

"Usually people who've been bullied," I said.

Stefon chewed some lettuce and nodded. "That makes sense. But the ghosts at The Kelpie...they could pick things up and throw them. Just like in the movie."

Stefon had personal knowledge of that. We all did. He couldn't see ghosts, but he sure could dodge when one of them flung a martini glass at his head.

"You're right. And that is very unusual...."

"But doesn't that make them poltergeists?" Stefon

interjected. "I asked about that at the time, but you all told me no. I thought I was vindicated."

Huh. Maybe he was right. This whole situation was making me question my assumptions. I'd have to ask the teens to do more research.

I didn't say any of that, though. I just shrugged and waved a hand near his chin, where spot of dressing had landed on his beard. Stefon wiped it away and sighed before picking up where he left off.

"I still don't get how all this hangs together. What does one thing have to do with another? And who is doing all of this?"

I shook my head and rose to put the kettle on. I really needed a cup of tea.

"I don't know."

But sure as I was formed in the image of the Goddess, I was going to find out.

11

———

It was another busy day at The Widening Gyre. The steady flow of customers had kept Duncan and me busy, which was good. It was a very good sales day, which we needed.

Tabitha and Tracy kept busy too, working on the new website and uploading three new T-shirt and mug designs. They had also convinced me to put some of the ghostly Biff-with-books designs on journals and notebooks.

Which was a really good idea. I even said so. Out loud.

The thing I didn't tell them was that I was probably going to want one of those dang notebooks for myself. They were on fire, those two. I had zero business acumen when I was in high school, and barely had any now. Where had they gotten this from? Tracy's mother, Carol? I mean, she was an accountant who ran her own business, but that's hardly what I think of as a classic entrepreneur.

At any rate, things had slowed down enough by late afternoon that I felt okay leaving Duncan to close up. So the teens and I piled into my pumpkin-orange electric Fiat and it was off to the Kelpie to talk to the ghosts.

I tried to sneak out to go on my own, but Tabitha and Tracy were having none of it, so all three of us were headed up the four-lane highway toward the old haunted inn.

The big wooden sign for the inn jutted out from above a brightly painted fence. It was quite artful, really. The sign depicted a black horse running across waves and the words The Historic Kelpie were written in fancy carved script. A red kraken emerged from the depths to grab the K. I pulled into the gravel parking lot that ran alongside the place, all the way back toward the towering trees that bordered the eccentric garden.

I was rather fond of The Kelpie, and had been visiting the place since I was a teen myself, just because it was so weird.

I unfolded myself from the front seat as Tracy and Tabitha scrambled out the other side. Two teenagers really shouldn't even fit back there, but they managed. Good thing they were skinny. No way would I fit in the backseat of a Fiat. Ever. Not with my ample and luscious frame. Yeah, I said it. Ample and luscious. I believed it, and so did my boyfriend. And that's all that mattered.

We headed through the parking lot to the back entrance, which led to a whimsical courtyard filled with plants, statues, and an old boat. The courtyard was formed by the two wings of the 1950s motel add-ons that, Liam, the owner, had turned into family suites with mini kitchens, small sitting rooms, and one to two bedrooms each. They were nice, and only slightly less haunted than the main—much older—three-story inn we were headed for.

A six-foot-long shark wearing a saddle sat on the porch. I patted the shark on the its snout before pushing through the heavy wooden doors set with stained glass. I was greeted as usual by the smell of popcorn from the old machine set up in the dusty, 1930s lobby. Boris Karloff leered down from an ancient television screen. The thing still showed videos on a VCR machine, for goodness sake.

"Hey Liam," I called out. "Are you here?"

"You." A condescending voice said. I looked up the stairs and it was our former local intrepid reporter, Chip Lancaster, with his soft, pasty pale face and a permanent scowl.

Chip lived at The Kelpie in exchange for interviewing the ghosts that also resided in the haunted inn. Chip was none too happy about the fact, since I had sentenced him to the task. Oh, it wasn't researching the ghosts that was the problem; he actually enjoyed that. It was the fact that I told him he had to publish any findings under the name *Anonymous*. Because it's not punishment if he can take credit, is it?

"Hi, Chip," I said, putting some extra pep in my words.

"What do you want?" he said, scowl deepening.

The teens scuffled on the carpet behind me. I didn't bother to look to see what the heck they were doing.

"I need to talk to Liam—is he around?"

"Heck if I know," Chip said, and disappeared back

up the stairs. I shrugged and followed the teens into the next room, which was a shadowy old bar with a long, shining vintage bar top.

Past that room was the big open dining room. Walking into that space was like walking into yet another time warp. Or an episode from that old TV show, *The Twilight Zone*. Sailboats and fish floats hung from the ceiling. A skeleton was propped in an old phone booth. Tables with built-in seats formed a horseshoe along the walls, and a long communal table took pride of place down the center. There was art, art everywhere. Strange art. Cowboys. Sailors. Nineteen seventies string art. Weird sculptures. An old jukebox. And framed paintings, hung floor to ceiling, and beyond.

I smelled coffee, and followed my nose through the swinging door to the old kitchen. The place had several microwaves for guests, one of which was considered haunted. No one could ever agree on which one, though. If it were up to me? I'd avoid them all.

Liam was making his famous thin pancakes at the stove, which was strange because not only were there no guests in the dining room, it was early evening. Well past breakfast time.

"Hi, Liam."

Liam is an Irish American in his early sixties, and still handsome as the day is long. He's run the inn and filled it with his collectibles since as long as I can remember.

"Hey Sarah, what are you doing here? Want some pancakes?"

"Cool!" said Tracy. "We want pancakes."

I rolled my eyes, but I couldn't disagree. Liam's

pancakes were the best. They were almost, but not quite, as thin as crepes and served with either butter and sugar or butter and syrup. I liked the butter and powdered sugar combo myself.

"I can't," I said. "But thanks."

The teenagers both looked at me with reproach, then both spoke simultaneously.

"Can we still have some?"

"Do we have time?"

"Yeah. I guess. All right." Just because I was meeting Stefon and Cyrus for dinner after this didn't mean I should deny growing teenagers the pleasure of Liam's pancakes.

"Pull up a stool," Liam said.

I looked around, and sure enough, four stools now sat near the counter, a new addition. We settled in. Liam expertly flipped pancakes onto plates. The smell hit me. My mouth watered. I had to prevent myself from snatching the top pancake from Tabitha's plate.

You're going to Costa's. Uncle Cyrus is paying. My mind said that. Sensible. Practical. My body disagreed.

The scent of the pancakes was really driving me bonkers. I squirmed on the hard metal stool.

"Why are you making pancakes again?" I asked.

"I was prepping batter for breakfast, and figured I'd make myself pancakes for dinner."

It made sense to me. I mean, why wouldn't a person eat the world's most delicious, thin, giant pancakes for dinner?

Liam smiled, then set a plate with the toddler-size pancake dusted with powdered sugar in front of me.

The teen's had gotten the full size versions that covered their entire plates.

"Looks like you were going to steal Tabitha's. Now you have your own. You can even have a fork." Liam set the utensil down in front of me.

"Thanks Liam. You know me too well."

Sure enough, the small pancake was heaven. I had to force myself to not shove the whole thing into my mouth at once.

"So," Liam said, once he had his own plate filled with three pancakes covered in melted butter. "What's up? Why are you here?"

I finished off my last bite and set the fork down firmly so that I wouldn't be tempted to snag anyone else's.

Dinner at Costa's. I reminded myself again. *No stealing anyone's pancakes.*

I cleared my throat. "I wanted to talk to the ghosts, but I figured I'd check in with you first, to let you know I'd be tromping around upstairs. Also, I wanted to ask if anything had been up with them lately. Have you noticed anything strange?"

Liam practically choked on his bite of pancake. "What isn't strange about the ghosts here? Holy moly."

He shook his head and squirreled another bite into his mouth. I let him chew.

"They have been coming downstairs more often lately, and not just to talk to Chip."

"How's that going, anyway?" Tracy piped in.

Now it was Liam's turn to shrug.

"It's okay; he's pretty low maintenance, and the ghosts definitely have seemed happier. Less rowdy and more content. So that's a good thing." He paused and looked my way. "Thanks for doing that, Sarah."

"Just doing my job," I replied. "But what else has been going on?"

"Well, you remember that main ghost at the center of last month's brouhaha?" Liam said around a bite of pancake. "The flapper?"

We all nodded.

"She's been coming downstairs a lot more lately, seeming like she wants to ask me a question. I asked Sophie to check in with her if she saw here while making up the rooms, but they haven't crossed paths yet. Maybe you should go talk to her...." He looked out the kitchen windows toward the garden and the weird, circus-themed chicken enclosure. "But do you mind telling me what this is about?"

I still wasn't clear on what the preferred protocol was regarding sharing magical information with civilians when Justice work was involved. But considering Liam had been at the center of my last case, and I was in his territory, asking to talk to one of the ghosts who lived here, it seemed only fair to spill.

"A bunch of things have gone missing lately, here and in Portland. We're not sure how widespread it is, or to what purpose..." What kind of language was that? Was becoming a Justice making me talk like I was an English teacher or something? Weird. "...but something pinged me to come here and talk to the ghosts. Most particularly because it turns out the ghosts at the big Hitchcock place in Portland have been agitated and something's missing from there."

"Biff said anything?" Liam asked.

I looked at Tracy and Tabitha, who both shook their heads, mouths filled with pancake.

"I guess that's a no," I said. "We also have a possible local poltergeist moved in, of the teenage human variety. So there's that too."

Liam frowned and scratched his chin. "I can't offer help on any of this, I'm afraid. But if you want to go up to the third floor and talk to the flapper, be my guest. You two done?"

The teens scraped their plates and reluctantly set down their forks.

"Yeah, I guess so," Tabitha replied.

"Can we help you clean up?" Tracy asked.

"I got it," Liam said. "You get along upstairs."

We shoved back from the counter and stood to go. Liam began stacking our plates.

"And Sarah." Liam stopped me. "You check in with me, you hear? If there's anything I need to know…"

"Sure thing, Liam. Thanks."

12

———

We climbed the back stairs at The Kelpie. You had to exit through the courtyard off the dining room and head through the garden to get to what was little more than a jumped-up fire escape. There was no longer a way to the top floor from inside the historic building, though there had been, once upon a time. People who stayed at The Kelpie told stories about ghosts climbing stairs that weren't there anymore, all dressed up, as if they were going dancing.

And sure enough, at the top of the clanging metal stairway was a speakeasy that had clearly been there since the 1930s. Last time I was here, the place was lively, filled with dancing ghosts and loud music. Today it was quiet. It felt almost deserted, which was strange.

Did ghosts take the day off? Did they sleep or something? There was so much I didn't know. So much I probably would never know. But that was okay. I needed to talk to only one ghost.

And there she was, sitting at the bar, a cup of coffee

in a old-fashioned white ceramic cup in front of her, one T-strap shoe dangling. The fascinator that was usually in her hair sat on the bar as well.

"Hey there."

She jerked up with a start, growing slightly more clear in front of my eyes. Her mascara was smudged as if she'd been up partying and drinking all night. That seemed strange too, but as I said, what do I know about ghosts?

"Can we talk to you for a moment?"

She grabbed my wrists, solidifying just for a second, and then her hands moved through me, leaving a cold patch. I surreptitiously rubbed at my wrists behind my back. It was the weirdest feeling, and one I didn't need to experience again.

::I'm so glad you're here,:: she said. *::I've been waiting for you.::*

"Did someone tell you I wanted to talk?"

Her gaze drifted away for a moment, as if she were confused.

::I'm not sure. But I wanted to see you.::

"Why is that?" I saw that both Tracy and Tabitha had out their phones and were taking notes. Probably a good idea. I wish I'd thought to ask them. Once again, the teens took initiative I didn't even know was needed.

::The ghosts in the area are upset.::

Both teens tapped away frantically. This was definitely new information. Ghosts communicating over distances? I'd never heard of it, and shot them both the look.

Their eyes were wide. At least I was keeping them

entertained on their summer break, giving them a strange paranormal education. Good thing Tracy's mother was a witch. But that reminded me: I had yet to meet Tabitha's parents. We'd have to change that sometime soon. They had to wonder what their offspring was up to.

::Are you paying attention?:: The flapper snapped her fingers in front of my nose. I could barely hear the snap, but it was startling all the same.

"Sorry, I just thought of something," I said. "So, the ghosts are agitated."

::Yes. Someone is taking objects we like. Things that mean something to us. Things that make us happy. They are spiriting them away.::

"Spiriting them away," I repeated. "What do you mean?"

My thoughts were racing again. Did that mean a noncorporeal being was our thief? Or was it something else?

::I don't know. All I know is they took Old Granddad's favorite watch and now he's sulking and won't move from the last spot he had it. Won't take any sustenance. Won't listen to the radio. He just kind of floats there in the corner by the stairs, facing the wall.::

I shivered. That sounded really creepy.

"I guess we need to check that out."

She turned her big sad eyes at me, the sharply cut bob framing her tense jawline.

::I guess you do. You are the Justice, after all. And you two...:: She turned to the teens, who both stopped typing into their phones and straightened up. They didn't look freaked out at her scrutiny, so points in their

favor. The flapper nodded, as if having some idea confirmed. ::*You two are good people. You help.*::

Then she turned back to her coffee, as if we were no longer there.

"Guess that's that," I said. "Let's go see if we can talk to this Old Granddad person."

"We have to?" Tracy asked, as we walked to the door and back out into the sunshine. Both teens looked a little queasy at the thought. As if the pancakes were turning in their stomachs. I didn't feel so good about it, either. I looked at my watch; almost time to meet Stefon and Uncle Cyrus for dinner.

Maybe we could put this part off. What's an extra day to a ghost, right? It's not as if they're in a hurry to get somewhere.

"Let me see what my uncle says," I replied. "We can always come back."

At least, that's what I told myself. In reality, the thought of facing Old Granddad gave me the cold spooky. And I really didn't want to know why, at least not yet.

Tabitha stopped, halfway down the metal stairs. "We're stalling. And you're the Justice."

Way to get to the point, kid. I sighed.

"Right on both counts, Tabitha. All right. Let's get this over with."

So it was down the outside stairs, back through the dining room, bar, and the small, art deco lobby with its popcorn smells, and up the carpeted stairs where Chip had oh so graciously told me to eff off.

At the top of the second floor landing, you could head two directions. Right took you to three bedroom suites and a kitchenette. Left took you through a parlor filled with more weird art, dark seascapes, and old low bookcases filled with art and books that squatted beneath large windows covered by lace curtains. Huge, overstuffed furniture was arranged in groupings for conversation or board games. An old ship captain stared down at me from an oil painting.

I didn't like the look in his eye. But I would rather look at him than where Tracy and Tabitha were staring, wide-eyed and open-mouthed.

Forcing myself to follow their gaze, I saw what must be Old Granddad. He wore an old, dark brown, 1940s suit, and a battered fedora crowned his head. His feet dangled, the tips of his shoes pointing toward the ground.

It reminded me of Fairuza Balk in *The Craft*.

The tiny pancake in my stomach flipped. I inhaled through my nose, trying not to sneeze at the dusty air. Out through my mouth.

Calm down, Sarah. It's just a ghost. Ghosts can't hurt you.

Except, I had solid proof that they could. Like, really solid. Like, throwing physical objects solid.

I forced myself to step toward the hovering spirit.

"Excuse me." My voice squeaked. I cleared my throat. "Old Granddad? We've come to ask about your watch."

The ghost slowly rotated, feet still dangling, toes toward the carpet. Silvery tears tracked down puffy pale cheeks, which were cratered and soft with age.

::Do you have it?::

"No. We're wondering where you last saw it. The woman upstairs told us it was missing."

As if she heard me, the flapper's legs emerged, one T-strap shoe at a time, heading down through the ceiling above us as if walking down a set of ghostly stairs, finally stepping far enough down that her head popped through the ceiling. The feathered fascinator was back in place around her sleek bobbed hair.

::Tell them, Pops.::

::I was heading upstairs to the party. I like the music. Big band. I paused here, on the stairs, to wind my watch, and...::

The teens and I leaned forward. Waiting.

The old ghost looked right at me. I shivered.

::A strange force wrenched it from my hand and broke the chain. Then my watch was simply...:: He made flicked his fingers and made a puffing shape with his mouth, *::...gone. Poof. Like a magic trick.::*

He looked up at the flapper then. She gazed at him with sympathy before floating farther down to stand next to him. Her shoes looked as if she was standing on a solid surface. So why were his shoes still in scary Fairuza Balk mode?

Ghosts. No telling with them, right?

::I miss my watch,:: he said.

::I know, Pops. But Sarah will get it back for you, won't you, Sarah?::

Gah. How in the world was I supposed to do that?

"We'll try to help," I temporized. "But there are a lot of other things missing, too. And we probably need to head to the Fuller Mansion. That's two hours out of town."

The flapper narrowed her eyes.

::You're going after the missing ring, aren't you?::

The teens gasped. I just stared. Why her words startled me, I don't know. Hadn't she told me upstairs that the ghosts were all communicating?

"You're going to research this whole ghosts-talking-at-a-distance-thing right?" I said, aiming my words sideways at the teens.

"Already noted," Tracy replied.

The flapper descended all the way to the floor and walked right up to me, placing one shivery-cold hand on my arm.

::If you're going to the mansion, I'm coming with you.::

"So are we," Tabitha replied.

"We're going to need a bigger car."

13

U ncle Cyrus had popped himself back to the mansion after dinner the night before, saying he had business to attend to before we arrived.

Since I didn't have the warlock's powers to apparate, or teleport, or whatever you wanted to call that danged annoying and convenient thing Cyrus did, I'd commandeered Stefon to drive the rest of us, leaving Duncan in charge of The Widening Gyre. Delta said she'd help out if he needed it. Leaving the shop on a summer's day was bad form, but needs must. Though I was going to have to have a talk with Uncle Cyrus about the wheres and hows of juggling being a small business owner and a Justice. I needed some serious strategies if this was going to continue.

Stefon navigated his SUV across the shining ribbon of the Willamette River. The Fuller Mansion sat just across the bridge in the southeast side of Portland. I rode shotgun, while the teens sat in the backseat, staring out the windows, sharing the occasional comment that I was only half paying attention to. The flapper flickered in and out of visibility between them.

"So," Stefon said. "Am I vindicated here? Are you now telling me the movie *Poltergeist* was right? That dead people do affect the physical world?"

"Well, of course they do," I said, voice a little sharp, "Just look around. This bridge was built by dead people."

I really didn't want to rehash this conversation. Mostly because I didn't have any good answers for him, and I hated that. I hate not knowing things.

Maybe that's why I've always read so much.

"Babe. Come on." He smoothly changed lanes. "You know that's not what I meant. And when I mentioned the movie before, you all treated me like some doofus."

I sighed, looking down at the sailboats, canvas bellied out with the wind, and two long scullers, skimming the surface of the water. A couple of seagulls wove and dodged in the sky.

"Sorry. That wasn't fair. And I don't mean to be cranky at you, either. It's just this whole case is under my skin. There's too much about it that I don't understand."

Stefon changed lanes again, passing a small red sports car, who, believe it or not, was driving too slowly for him.

"Isn't that the way life always is, though? We approach things we don't understand. We learn something new. Figure stuff out."

"I guess so," I replied. "But, you know, all my magical training taught me to believe that poltergeists were just teenagers coming into their powers and lacking control. But then…"

"But then," Stefon interjected, "a ghost threw a martini glass at my head a few months ago now, didn't they?"

I laughed. Yeah, he was right about that. Those ghosts threw a lot more than martini glasses. They were having a regular fit at The Historic Kelpie. And what did it mean that we had a ghost in the car, right now?

And speaking of which… I looked over my shoulder. Sure enough, there she was. Looking back at me.

"Hey, Tabitha," I said.

"Yeah?"

"That's another thing to add to your notes, and the book I guess you two are going to have to write, updating all the knowledge we have about ghosts."

"What's that?" Tracy said.

"Ghosts can cross water."

"Oh, cool." Tabitha replied.

"You're right!" Tracy said.

::*Of course we can,*:: the flapper interjected, her voice ringing loud and clear inside my head. ::*Where do you living humans get your strange ideas from anyway?*::

She scoffed in disgust and then winked out again, leaving an empty spot in the back seat.

"I really wish she would either stay or go," Tracy said. "She's kind of freaking me out."

::*Too bad,*:: the ghost said, even though the flapper herself was nowhere to be seen.

Stefon cleared his throat. "So, poltergeists."

I took up the thread again as he navigated off the bridge and onto a narrow side street.

"Well, if ghosts can cross water, throw things, and communicate with each other over long distances, then all bets are off. And clearly, I don't know anything about ghosts."

"That's not true," Tabitha said. "You're just refining your data points."

"Yeah," Tracy said encouragingly. "Data points."

It was sweet. The teens thought I needed reassurance. Maybe I did.

"All I know right now," I said, "is that I'm glad I have the three of you to help me."

And everyone else in Seashell Cove, I thought. The nice thing about coming into my own as a witch, and taking on the mantle of Justice, was the realization that I didn't have to go it alone. And as a matter of fact, everyone was better off if I didn't.

"Teamwork makes the dream work," I muttered.

"Babe." Stefon said, "Corporate speak?"

I laughed again. And then gasped.

"Holy moly, Stefon, you've been holding out on me."

Above us on its own small hill stood an amazing, stately mansion. The place was a giant Queen Anne Victorian wedding cake with turrets and arched, carved balustrades framing a gracious front porch that wrapped most of the way around. The three-story building was a rich blue with white trim so bright it gleamed in the sun.

"This place is amazing," Tabitha said.

"I totally want to live here," Tracy replied.

I didn't blame them. I did too, except I didn't want to spend that much time cleaning. I had enough trouble keeping my cozy bungalow tidy with the hours I worked. Though I guessed anyone who lived in a house like this had staff to take care of things like dusting and cleaning toilets.

Stefon turned the corner into a tiny parking area that faced the back of the mansion.

"Well, here we are," he said, exiting the SUV. "The beautiful Fuller Mansion, built in 1892 by an exploitive lumber baron."

"Everything always comes at a cost, doesn't it?" I replied, stretching my back.

"That's for sure," Tabitha said, climbing out.

"Are we going in?" Tracy asked, "or are we just gonna stand here and stare at this beautiful building?"

Suddenly, the flapper was in front of the car, hands on her skinny, boyish hips, tapping one T-strap shoe toe.

"Guess we're going in," I said, as the flapper turned with a swirl of beads and fringe and headed toward the gate leading to the home of Elias Fuller, ghost.

14

———————

Stepping inside the mansion took my breath away. The place was a Victorian marvel.

We were greeted by a large foyer and tiled fireplace with a winged Isis fire screen in front. Peacock wallpaper adorned the walls and a carved walnut balustrade swept up the stairs leading to the second floor. Leaded glass winked above wood-framed double-hung windows.

All of this made way to more gleaming hardwood floors, and a giant red- and blue- patterned carpet supporting a three-legged table with a guest book and brochures arrayed on it. Through a cased opening to my right was a long room with a second fireplace surrounded with elaborate tiles that showed scenes of workers laying railroad tracks and tall Douglas fir trees towering on each side, picked out in green glaze.

I punched Stefon's arm lightly. "Now I really can't believe you never took me here."

"I was getting there, babe. I told you." His voice was reverent.

"This place is awesome!" Tracy exclaimed.

"Holy cow," Tabitha whispered. "I've never seen anything like this."

I was just as awed.

"Are we supposed to check in or something?" I asked Stefon.

He shrugged his broad shoulders. "I don't know. I've only ever been here at holiday time for official events. I have no clue what goes on on a regular day."

And then, floating down the stairs was a dapper man in loose trousers and a crisp white shirt beneath a waistcoat and what I guessed was called a frock coat. He had a thin, narrow face. His dark hair was slicked back, his face clean-shaven.

Whoever he was, he was clearly a white man of means. He was also equally clearly a ghost.

In my head I heard the flapper gasp.

::*Elias*,:: she said, staring upward at him, transfixed.

::*Bunny*,:: he replied, voice reverent.

Oh great. I turned to the flapper.

"Really? This is why you wanted to come? And here I thought you were worried about the missing objects. And isn't he a little old for you?"

She sniffed and raised one slender shoulder. ::*I am worried about the missing objects. I want to help you.*::

"But you also knew Elias Fuller was here. Didn't you, Bunny?" I should've known her name was Bunny. Flappers always had the strangest names. Not that someone whose middle name was Endora could talk. Thanks, Mom and Dad.

Bunny cast her eyes down, but her lips quirked in wily smirk. Great. Just what I needed, to be involved in some sort of ghostly love affair.

"Sarah."

I turned. Uncle Cyrus stood in a carved doorway, flanked by two elaborate pocket doors. He fit the place a lot better than our ragtag group in sneakers and jeans. Bunny excepted, of course. Today he wore his usual crisp shirt—this one in small checks—beneath a sharp navy suit. And navy shoes that I knew for a fact were made from Italian leather.

I walked towards him, leaving the teens behind. Stefon was engrossed with the fireplace tiles. Anything to do with history, that's my man, even though I knew he'd seen that fireplace a thousand times. Come to think of it though, he probably hadn't seen it without a crush of people standing in front of it. Hmm. I guess there were advantages to me being Justice after all. I got to treat my boyfriend to an impromptu tour of an empty mansion.

As I walked towards Cyrus, I smelled his signature Bay Rum and frankincense combination. It was the scent of my childhood, and even when I was annoyed at him, it calmed me.

"Have you found anything out?" I asked. He shook his head, then looked past my shoulder.

"You brought a ghost."

"She insisted on coming." I glanced up the stairs. Sure enough, stopped halfway were Elias and Bunny, though I had a hard time thinking of her as that name. I wondered if it was just his affectionate term for her.

"I thought she wanted to help," I said, "I didn't realize I was playing ghostly matchmaker."

Uncle Cyrus laughed. "Ghostly romance. Gets you every time, I guess."

"Can you show me where the ring is missing from?"

"Sure can. But Elias there knows more about it than I do."

"And?" I said, raising an eyebrow.

"And he hasn't been talking. But maybe now that your ghost is here to soften him up, he'll help us more."

He'd said before that Masons had no truck with warlocks and witches, which I didn't understand. But everyone has their prejudices, I guess.

"I'm going with Cyrus," I called back to the teens and Stefon. "You can explore or come with."

They all jerked their heads toward me, as if having forgotten why we were even there. All three followed, leaving Bunny and Elias to their wooing.

Cyrus led us into a side room. And by side room I mean a vast place with fourteen-foot-high ceilings, crown molding, carved window ledges, and more glass. And best of all, there were floor-to-ceiling bookcases with two library ladders. And another fireplace. Oh my gosh, be still my beating witchy heart.

Along with the bookcases that I was itching to explore were several groupings of comfortable-looking upholstered leather chairs and small tables, placed here and there throughout the room on jewel-like carpets. The chairs were all filled with ghosts.

"Whoa, that's a lot of ghosts," Tabitha said.

"There's ghosts?" Stefon asked, head swiveling.

"Yeah, everywhere. You might not want to sit in any of the chairs," Tracy said.

Uncle Cyrus led me toward an elaborate frame between two of the bookcases. It was a shadow box with a heavily embroidered and beaded apron with velvet trim inside.

"Is this one of those aprons you were talking about?" Stefon asked.

"Yep. That's a Masonic apron, all right," I replied. "It's pretty nice. If you like playing dress-up."

Stefon shot me a look. Oops. "I love it when you play dress-up, Stefon."

And I did. He's hot as all get out in a tunic and armor. He didn't look like he was buying it, though.

I'd just have to make it up to him somehow. Later.

Like, after we'd cracked this case.

15

———

"Sarah, there's someone here I'd like you to meet," Uncle Cyrus said. An Asian woman with long dark hair caught up in a neat bun at the base of her neck stepped forward.

She looked as neatly put together as my uncle, wearing black pants, black wing tip shoes, and a burgundy blazer over a white crisp blouse. I was starting to wonder if I needed to up my clothing game if I was going to live my life as a full-fledged witch and Justice. But whatever, jeans and T-shirt would have to do for now, wouldn't they?

"Sarah, this is Ah Lam Wu. Ah Lam, my niece, Sarah Endora Braxton."

I winced at his use of my middle name.

"It's a pleasure to meet you, Sarah. I've heard much about you over the years."

I raised an eyebrow. "Really?"

I hadn't heard a thing about her, which I did not mention.

"Uncle Cyrus doesn't talk much about his work to me," was what I said. "But it's nice to finally meet one of his colleagues."

She nodded and smiled. "We do tend to be a secretive bunch. Security culture, you know."

I smiled and acted like I knew what she was talking about.

"Tell you later," Stefon whispered. Great, that meant I must look as confused as I felt.

"I would offer you a chair, but..." She swept an elegant hand around the room.

"They are all occupied aren't they?" Stating the obvious, Sarah.

"Indeed."

"We need to find somewhere to talk," Uncle Cyrus said. "Sarah and the others have news from Seashell Cove."

And, almost as if they had heard him, four ghosts sitting at one of the round tables stood, adjusted their frock coats and skirts, and glided from the room.

"Quick!" said Ah Lam Wu. "Grab the seats before more ghosts show up!"

We scrambled for the table as Stefon looked around the room.

"Any spare chairs at the other tables?" he asked the teens. "I don't want to steal one if its occupied."

The girls located two more chairs and helped carry them over.

Once we were seated, Ms. Wu looked around. "I wonder where Mr. Fuller has gotten to."

"Oh." I snorted. "I know exactly where he is. He's making time with Bunny. Pitching woo."

Her smooth brow wrinkled. "Bunny?"

"Yeah. A ghost we brought with us."

"A ghost. You brought with you." She looked at me as if I was bonkers.

"She rode with us in the car," Tabitha chimed in.

"It was kind of weird," said Tracy. "She kept flickering in and out. And did you know that ghosts can cross water?"

Ms. Wu looked at the teens, and then back at me.

"I'm quite impressed. You must be a very powerful witch to be able to transport a ghost."

I shrugged. I seemed to be doing a lot of that this trip.

"I don't think I had anything to do with it. Nothing was going to get in the way of Bunny and her love, Elias Fuller. So, what do you know?"

"Well, since I last spoke with your uncle, not only is the star ruby ring missing, but so is the Master's Trowel."

I was certain Elias Fuller had never laid brick or tile in his life, but what do I know about Masonic rituals?

"That's a lot of things missing," said Tracy, "but I still don't get it."

I didn't get it either.

"Who, what, and why would be taking such a strange combination of tools?" I said. "That's the question we have to answer."

::*I think I know,*:: a ghostly voice said in our heads. Everyone looked towards the doorway, except Stefon, who looked at me, confused.

"What's happening?" he said. "Where's everyone looking?"

"Fuller and Bunny just showed up," I muttered.

Elias Fuller strode confidently across the room, Bunny trailing in his wake.

::*Welcome to my home,*:: he said when he approached the table. ::*I see more witches have arrived. I always had a soft spot in my heart for witches. Especially witches wearing those new-fangled dungarees.*::

He practically leered at me when he said that. Gross. Bunny smacked him with her clutch purse.

::*Elias. Behave yourself.*::

::*And why would I want to do that, my dear? What's the fun in it?*::

He wrapped an arm around her waist and whispered in her ear.

Bunny giggled. ::*You're incorrigible.*::

I had to admit, hearing ghosts flirting inside my head was very unnerving and not something I ever cared to experience again. I mean, I'm no prude—just look at my history—but come on. Get a room.

"What's happening now?" Stefon whispered. "You like like you sucked on a lemon."

"I'll tell you later. Suffice to say, Elias Fuller is a bit of a sexist creep."

Stefon scowled and began to push back his chair. I tugged at his arm and gave him a look. He grumbled, but settled down.

::*I have done some investigation,*:: Fuller said, growing somber again. ::*There is a powerful warlock....*:: He looked to Uncle Cyrus.

"Dead or alive?" my uncle asked.

Elias stroked his chin thoughtfully. ::*That, I do not know. All I know is the signature of the magic.*::

"Male or Female?" Ms. Wu asked.

"Or neither?" I chimed in.

::I cannot get the flavor of that either.::

"But you're sure it's a warlock, and not some other magical being?" I asked.

::That is one thing I am sure of. I would stake my life on it. If I were still alive.:: Laughter rumbled from his chest and belly. He must have been quite the raconteur when he was alive, if he was this way after death.

And I bet his housemaids weren't safe. Ugh.

Bunny just smiled, tilting her head toward his. *::Aren't you a card?::*

"I don't get it," Tracy said. "How can you tell the difference between a witch's and a warlock's magical signature?"

Uncle Cyrus explained. "Witches work with the basic elements, often developing a stronger relationship with one or two of them. They also tend to focus on primarily one psychic skill, though they can draw upon any element, and some witches have been known to master several psychic skills in their lifetimes. Warlocks? Along with having an affinity with the natural elements, we also have the ability to shift space and time."

Both teens rapidly typed the information into their phones, as if Cyrus was dispensing pearls of wisdom. I really liked having those two around for research. Less work for me.

Then it struck me. "So, maybe it isn't Jerry Hamamoto after all. Jerry is a witch, not a warlock."

"I told you he was okay, babe," Stefon said, squeezing my hand.

"But this is worse," I said, "because now we're back at square one. Either I have no suspects, or Mr. Hamamoto is working with a warlock."

I turned Ms. Wu.

"How are we going to find the culprit?"

She held my gaze with clear, steady eyes. Her energy was calm, cool and certain—a lot like Uncle Cyrus's, come to think of it.

"You are not alone, Sarah. You are never alone."

Her eyes took on a bright cast, and her energy shifted slightly, as if some sort of strange prophecy was coming through her. I'd seen it happen with both witches and warlocks before, and since I became Justice, it was happening to me more and more often.

I willed my breathing to slow down, and settled deeper into my center, placing both feet flat on the carpeted floor. Stefon went into what I think of as warrior mode beside me, turning into a solid mountain, but ready to move at any moment. Everyone at the table felt poised, breathless.

"You are never alone, witch Sarah. Even in the darkest times. Even in the midst of danger. Even when the waters feel as if they will close above your head. You are never alone. All you have to do is call upon us. Every witch and every warlock within distance will come to your aid. You must call upon the power of the Star Goddess. She who connects us all. She who is eternal. She who is both death and life and death and life again."

She reached out and grabbed one of my hands. Her fingers felt like ice.

"Never give up, Sarah Endora Braxton. Never. Give. In."

She dropped my hand and shuddered, then closed her eyes and sank back into her chair. Everyone at the table was still. Even Bunny and Mr. Fuller had stopped their flirting and stood ramrod straight, waiting.

Finally, Ah Lam blinked three times and inhaled deeply. I swear, all of us with corporeal bodies inhaled at the same time.

"Well," she said, voice dry. "That was interesting."

She looked at Uncle Cyrus. "Some family you have, my dear."

He grinned. "Indeed, I have quite the family, and I couldn't be prouder."

I sniffed back a tear, and Stefon squeezed my shoulders.

"See, babe. Everything's gonna be all right."

I hoped against hope that he was right. It might have felt that way in the moment. But long term? I wasn't so sure.

16

———

After Ah Lam Wu did her whole psychic stream of consciousness thingy, we had settled into discussing the variety of missing objects, and the lack of possible suspects. Bunny and Elias Fuller were soon bored, and took off to canoodle somewhere.

Soon enough, we had piled back into Stefon's SUV with Uncle Cyrus promising to meet us for dinner in Seashell Cove later, saying he still had more business to attend to.

I wondered if part of his business was courting Ms. Wu. If so, I couldn't blame him. She was a middle-aged hottie, which is something I aspire to be myself someday.

"Okay," Stefon said, "let me figure out how to get back onto the bridge from here."

He navigated his way out the driveway and down the twisty streets. Finally making a hard right and heading back by the railroad tracks toward the bridge that would take us cross the Willamette River.

I heard sniffling in the back seat and looked over my shoulder, only to find both the teenagers looking sympathetic and concerned at the sobbing ghost in the middle seat.

"Something wrong, babe?" Stefon asked.

"Bunny seems to be upset about something." Though I couldn't figure out what the heck could have happened. They had both seemed so cozy. As a matter of fact, I'd expected Bunny to stay behind at the mansion.

But seriously, we had all been talking in that amazing library room in the mansion, and had gone off to a smaller room to examine some Masonic tools and artifacts. Partially from interest, and partially to give Bunny and Elias Fuller a bit more time together. And now here we were, with a flapper having the vapors in the back seat of my boyfriend's car.

I tried to not groan. Really, I did. But I had not signed up for this.

"Bunny?" Tabitha asked, voice tentative. "Is there something we can do to help?"

The ghost sniffed louder. Drawing a white hankie from her clutch purse, she noisily blew her nose. And let me tell you, if you've never had a ghost blow their nose basically inside your head? It's very creepy and mildly uncomfortable. It was a disturbing thing that I hoped would never happen again.

Honk. I winced, and tried to school my face back into a sympathetic guise.

"Bunny?" I asked realization finally dawning. "Did Mr. Fuller say something to upset you?"

::*He said he was moving on. It was over. After all I've
done for him, the rat!*::

"What do you mean, after all you've done for him?"

::*I can't tell you! I promised!*:: she said, and burst back
into tears.

The teens both looked at me.

I have no idea, I mouthed, then cleared my throat.
"Well, if you decide you need our help, just let us know.
Okay?"

The course of true love never did run smooth, I
guessed. They had seemed so into each other when we
arrived. When had they argued?

And what exactly was the flapper hiding from us?
The fact that she didn't want to tell me what exactly she'd
done for Elias Fuller was mildly disturbing, but with this
case and all, I didn't really have time to focus on it.

I turned back around, leaving the flapper to the
ministrations of the teens. Stefon had found his route
to the bridge and we were already halfway over the
water. The sun was still high in the sky. Sailboats still
sailed and scullers still skimmed the water, but somehow, the river did not look as kind as it had on our way
here. I wondered why.

All I knew was it was going to be a long two hours if
Bunny kept blowing her nose.

Honk.

Not for the first time, I wished I had a warlock's
ability to pop in and out wherever I wanted to. I
wondered if that was a skill that could be taught, or if it
was just something warlocks knew how to do.

"Hey, Tracy?"

"Yeah?" she called out from the back seat.

"Can you make a note that I need to ask Uncle Cyrus more about how he pops in and out of places?"

"Sure," she said.

"It is seriously cool," Tabitha replied. "We've been studying apparating and teleportation ever since we met him. But I think most of the things that have been written on it are pure speculation. Are there books that warlocks and witches have written that we could reference?"

She kept her voice light and innocent, but I knew exactly what she was fishing for. Both teens had asked me this question before, and I had evaded it. Partially because I didn't want them clamoring to access materials they weren't ready for, and partially because, frankly, I still didn't know the half of it.

"I don't really know," I said, just as innocently. "Maybe you can ask Cyrus about that, too."

I grinned inside, feeling slightly evil. But that's all right. Uncle Cyrus deserved it. He needed to be kept on his toes.

Stefon turned to me and smirked. "Babe."

"What? They should ask him, don't you think?" I widened my eyes. "He's the expert."

Stefon just smirked again, and turned his eyes back to the road.

"All right, get us home, Jeeves," I said.

"Will do, Mr. Wooster."

"Who are you talking about?" Tabitha asked. "Are those more magic people we should look up?"

Stefon and I both laughed.

"Oh, they're a certain kind of magic, all right,"

Stefon replied. "And you should definitely read up on them."

Bunny wailed. ::*How can you laugh when my heart is breaking? After Elias Fuller's betrayal?*::

All four of us groaned.

Like I said. It was going to be a long ride. Good thing Uncle Cyrus was paying for dinner again. We were going to need it.

Meanwhile, though, I might as well ask some more questions.

"Tabitha, are you ever going to bring your parents to the shop to meet me? Don't they want to see where you spend so much time?"

I could practically feel her squirming behind me. Tough Goth Wiccan girl was uncomfortable.

"She can't," Tracy said.

"And why is that?" I purposely kept my eyes on the road, rather than looking at Tabitha. We were on the highway, heading southwest now. The city traffic had cleared and Stefon was making good time.

"I can't tell you," Tabitha blurted.

Great. Another secret. This time, I did turn. The teen's usually olive-toned skin was ashy and pale. She looked scared.

"Tabitha? Is everything okay with your parents? Are *you* okay?"

She looked down at her lap, where her hands were clutching each other so hard, her knuckles were turning white.

Tracy reached across the ghost and laid a reassuring hand on Tabitha's arm.

"It's okay, Tab. You don't have to tell her. But I think

you probably should. She'll be cool, just like my mom."

Tabitha looked up at me, eyes stricken.

"Tabitha, whatever it is, we'll get through it together. Like we always do. Right, Stefon?"

"That's right. Whatever it is? We got your back."

"Go ahead," Tracy urged. "It's time."

The air in the car was thick with emotion. It felt as if Tabitha was going to burst out of her skin.

::Why isn't anyone paying attention to me?:: Bunny wailed. *::I'm the one in pain, here!::*

"Not now, Bunny!" we all said at once.

She sniffed, but fell silent.

Tabitha swiped at her eyes. I saw her squeeze Tracy's hand, who let go and settled back in her own space again. That was probably more comfortable for both Bunny and Tracy. Tracy's arm must be freezing where it had rested against the ghost's lap.

Tabitha looked at me, then out the window, then back again.

"If it helps, you can close your eyes and tell me," I said.

"You...you've never met my parents because..."

She swallowed. I forced myself to breathe and be patient.

"They only come out at night."

Stefon hummed the next line of Hall and Oates' "Maneater" very softly. I poked him. Hard. Now was not the time.

"What are you trying to tell me?" I asked.

She looked at me again, seeming a little steadier this time.

"My parents are both vampires."

17

Cyrus had met us at Costa's, managing to finagle a window table. The ocean view was spectacular, and one of my favorite things about Seashell Cove.

Costa's restaurant is at the Seaside Hotel, Seashell Cove's one slightly upscale place to stay. Most tourists booked a room in one of the guest houses or motels dotting the highway. But if you could afford the views? Why would you stay anywhere but the Seaside?

At least, that's what Cyrus always said, though why someone who could pop to Paris at will would stay in Seashell Cove in the first place, I wasn't sure. Regardless, I was glad he now had a home on the fancy outskirts of Portland, so I could easily visit him when I wanted to.

Stefon had his usual local IPA; Uncle Cyrus, a glass of pinot noir; and I was nursing one of my current summer favorites, a Spanish Albariño. When Uncle Cyrus is buying, I get the best. The large windows currently framed a vee of pelicans flying over the ocean, and the ubiquitous kites—bright box kites, dragons, and fish—flapping on the ends of their long strings.

Sunset wouldn't be for a bit yet, but hopefully, we'd still be here, enjoying dessert as the sun went down.

"Anything happen on the way home?" Uncle Cyrus asked, setting down his glass. Tonight, Cyrus wore a crisp white button-down shirt that I'm sure came from some expensive Italian designer. The sleeves were rolled up to expose the rich brown skin of his arms, and the dome of his head was completely smooth, as always. Stefon wore a plain black T-shirt for once, as did I. They were our concession to dressing up during the summer. I was also trying out a new pair of linen trousers that Stefon said made my butt look great. But then, he said that about everything I wore. It was part of why I kept him around.

I picked up my own glass and sniffed the crisp apple scent of it. "Bunny had a meltdown in the car. I guess Elias Fuller dumped her."

Something about that still didn't sit right with me, but since I had nothing concrete to point to, I decided not to mention it. Why muddy the waters with ghostly drama?

Taking a sip, I rolled the wine across my tongue. Outside the window, an osprey plummeted toward the ocean, diving for dinner.

"Oh, and Tabitha confessed that her parents are vampires."

"That is...interesting."

"I thought there was supposed to be some sort of magical registry or something. Why are there all these new magical beings in Seashell Cove? Does this sort of thing happen often?"

Uncle Cyrus picked up his glass again and swirled the ruby liquid around the bowl, looking thoughtful.

"It does seem that magical activity has increased in the past year. We'll have to look into why. Perhaps it's astrological. But for now? We need to focus on this case. Once it's done, I can help you interview the magical beings. Take a local census, perhaps. There hasn't been a proper one done in at least a decade."

A server set down a basket of warm rosemary bread and whipped butter, along with a small dish of green olives. Stefon and I both dove in as Cyrus watched, amused.

"So what's the deal at the mansion?" Stefon asked, after swallowing his last bite of bread. "All the times I've been there, I've noticed the Masonic details in the carvings and stuff, but never saw any of the actual regalia."

"It is beautiful," Uncle Cyrus said. "A lot to maintain, though. But to answer your question, the regalia is kept in rooms off-limits to all but practicing Masons. And those of us in the magical community whom the Masons have reason to trust. Ah Lam and I spent some time there after you left. Elias Fuller and another Mason joined us. Apparently Elias's ring had been in his family for two generations. He didn't have any offspring to leave it to, which is how his home and collection ended up being stewarded by the trust that runs the Fuller Mansion."

"So, what's the deal with you and Ah Lam Wu? She's pretty hot." I snagged a green olive from the dish in the center of the table.

"Ms. Wu and I are colleagues and have worked together on magical disturbances in the past. She is a very attractive warlock, but we are not involved. Not that it is any of your business."

I took a thoughtful sip of wine. Did I detect a slightly ruddy cast to Uncle Cyrus's face? But he was right, it wasn't my business.

The server arrived with our dinners. I had trout with vegetables, and so did Stefon. Uncle Cyrus got a rare steak. I never quite understood the appeal of coming to a seafood restaurant and eating cow—let alone barely cooked—but to each their own.

"You part vampire?" I asked Cyrus, gesturing at his plate.

"Very funny. No. I am not."

We focused on our dinner and the view for a while, but something poked at the back of my mind. Bothering me.

"Uncle Cyrus, what else are you keeping from me?"

His hands stilled, fork and knife poised over his plate. "What do you mean?"

"You didn't tell me about the tarot witch or the vampires. What else do you know that you aren't telling me? As Justice, I need to know."

I shoved a bit of trout in my mouth, but barely tasted it.

He sighed, and set down his utensils with a clink. "One of the reasons I came to town was to talk with you about Mr. Hamamoto. I told you that."

"And the vampires? You knew about them, didn't you? And you didn't tell me."

He held up his hands to ward me off. "I only

suspected. It was the third reason I came to town. To see if there was any truth to the rumors."

"But isn't that Sarah's job?" Stefon asked. "As Justice? Like, shouldn't she be on the inside of all this by now?"

"You don't understand..." Cyrus began.

Stefon shook his head. "I think I do, and I think it's kind of whack. Your old boy's club, or whatever it is, gives Sarah all this responsibility, but then still treats her like a child. Yeah. Whack."

He angrily stabbed at his vegetable medley while Cyrus and I stared at him, jaws slack. Stefon is usually pretty even tempered, but, don't wake the mama bear, I guess.

It's funny. Uncle Cyrus has been a mentor to me my whole life. But in the last year or so since I've been trying to grow into my witchy responsibilities, and especially since I took on the mantle of Justice, it felt as if we'd been more at odds. I didn't like it. And I was still a little pissed off by it, too.

As if he heard my thoughts. Uncle Cyrus reached a hand across the table, stopping halfway across, next to the salt and pepper shakers.

I paused, then reached my fingers toward him, touching his smooth, warm skin. I swear, the man's nails are always manicured to within an inch of their lives. Unlike mine.

"I know it's been rough for you," he said, "and it feels as if I'm pulling away. And hiding things."

"Aren't you?"

"Everyone has to go through this at your age, Sarah. Every witch, every warlock. Every magician. We all get eased into our roles, and information gets doled out, sometimes more slowly than is comfortable. But we have to make sure you can handle things on your own, and not dump too much information on you all at once."

"I'm doing just fine," I groused. Taking a gulp of wine too fast, I started coughing. I jerked my hand away from my uncle to do the old cough-in-your-elbow trick as Stefon rubbed my back. Uncle Cyrus's hand remained in the middle of the table, still offering friendship and goodwill.

I pretended I didn't notice.

"It's not that I don't want to help you, Sarah. Or tell you all the things. It's just part of the rules. As I said, we all go through it, just like a doctor goes through residency."

Stefon shook his head. Still not buying it.

I wiped my mouth and shoved my plate away. "So, this really happens to everyone in the first year after they pass their test?"

Cyrus nodded.

"Is it just a year? Or more? How long can I expect to have partial backup and only half the information I need?"

Okay, I guess I was still feeling a bit stung and defensive.

"A year and a day," Cyrus said.

"And then what happens?" Stefon asked. "She gets knighted or something?"

Cyrus and I both stared at him again, and I'm sure I looked just as confused as my uncle.

"Well, supposedly she's already Justice around here,

but you're still treating her as if she's an apprentice, or a squire. So I thought maybe you all had other titles you throw around. Or are there levels of Justice, like the Masons have? Or in martial arts. Like, are you a tenth-degree Justice, or something?"

He looked at Cyrus with a mixture of interest and anger on my behalf. It only made me love him more.

"You know, that isn't so far off," Uncle Cyrus mused, picking up his wine glass again. "And frankly, it's a good idea. To make the levels of the office of Justice more distinct, so people have a better sense of what they still need to learn."

"You think?" I asked. Now it was my turn to shake my head. "But let's table this part of the conversation for now. We still need to figure out what's happening with all the stolen goods."

I looked around for the server. "And I could really use a piece of cake."

18

────────

I pulled my little orange Fiat into the parking lot next to The Widening Gyre. It was a small parking lot, but it was all our own, and useful, especially for the colder rainy season when there was less foot traffic and people wanted to drive. During summer, it was mostly empty.

Locking up my car, I noticed that the soil around the planters was damp. Good. Duncan must have watered before he left the day before, giving it a good soaking. I fished my keys out of my bag and paused. Outside the door, something else caught my eye. In the planter box closest to the door... What was it?

I bent closer to the low bushes and bright white, orange, and purple flowers. They were pretty, but don't ask me their names. I gave Duncan free rein with the planter boxes because I don't have the patience to learn. But what had I seen?

There. Sure enough, marked in the soil, were footprints. One was what looked like the front half of a large running shoe, but the others were some sort of animal I didn't recognize. It wasn't squirrel. Too big. I didn't think it was a raccoon. I was used to those prints around my house.

But it was something similar to a raccoon.... What could it be? I snapped a photo of both sets of prints and unlocked the store, bells jangling.

Rhiannon ran toward me, meowing.

"Hello, Rhiannon. Good morning. I guess you want your breakfast, don't you?"

::Of course I do. Why wouldn't I? But that's not why I'm talking to you right now.::

I sighed and turned to re-lock the door.

"Follow me," I said, making my way back towards the small kitchen and break room next to the even smaller washroom.

"What's been happening?" I asked as I flicked on the kitchen lights. First things first, I filled the electric kettle and switched it on. Priorities. Second, I rummaged for Rhiannon's kibble and refilled her water dish. She pranced about my feet like a dog, which was unusual. Usually she waited patiently by her bowls, but this time, she was still looking up at me instead of diving for the kibble nuggets.

"Rhiannon, what's the matter?" I got down my favorite blue-glazed mug from Bart's shop and started preparing the Brown Betty pot to brew some strong English Breakfast tea.

::We had visitors last night.::

"Visitors," I repeated. "They the ones that left the footprints outside?"

::I guess so.::

"Did you recognize them?"

::One of them was human. Tall. But I couldn't see their face very clearly. They wore a hat that shaded their face, even in those obnoxious lights you put up outside. They rattled the doorknob.::

"And the other? I noticed animal prints," I said, swirling hot water inside the brown glazed teapot to prime it.

::It was largish. I could see its face just fine.::

"What kind of animal?" The last thing I needed was a coyote or some other predator around. We even had the occasional mountain lion come down from the hills, though the prints outside were not cat of any kind.

::It was a rabbit,:: she said. *::It looked like a wererabbit. Teeth, you know. And glowing eyes.::* She bent to crunch some kibble.

I sputtered. "A rabbit? Are you kidding me? We don't have rabbits around here, and I thought you said it was largish. And a wererabbit? Come on, Rhiannon."

::I know what I saw.:: Rhiannon sniffed, then bent back to her kibble and wouldn't say any more.

Since Rhiannon wasn't talking, and the store didn't open for half an hour, I took my mug of tea back to the paranormal section to see if I could find anything useful about missing magical objects. En route, I spied a couple of books that needed reshelving.

I really wished customers would either put things back in their proper place or just bring them to the front counter. But that was the way retail went: you had to pick up after the tourists. At least some of them spent money.

I turned on the floor lamp in the corner near the cozy chair, and started scanning the shelves as I sipped my tea.

"Hey, Biff," I said. "You ever heard anything about wererabbits?" I didn't get a response. Sometimes Biff appeared, sometimes he didn't, depending on his ghostly mood, I guessed. He certainly showed up more regularly these days, but was quiet right now. Turns out Biff wasn't a morning ghost.

I got up and snagged *Legends of Vampires and Werewolves* and set that down on the chair, then kept looking, mug of tea in hand. I thought about texting Tabitha and Tracy, but they were set to come in later anyway. Besides, I needed to start learning how to do some of this research on my own.

"What else?" I looked down the shelves, scanning the multicolored spines, then had a thought. I grabbed the book in my non-tea holding hand and headed to the children's section. I had remembered a favorite book from my own childhood. Both my parents thought it was hilarious, but they indulged me. I hoped I had a copy on hand. Maybe in the used section....

I scanned the shelves, and there it was, in all its strange, paperback glory: *Bunnicula*. I smiled, looking at the cover of the rabbit with very sharp teeth, and added it to my stack. I took both books back to the counter, climbed up on a high stool, and settled in to read. I still had a few minutes before I had to open up; might as well use the time wisely.

There was a knock on the door. Peering through the glass, gray hair wild as usual, was Delta Crabbit, with Preston the gnome riding on her shoulder.

Wow. Not only had those two become fast friends, but she was getting more and more lax about hiding him in public lately.

I unlocked the door and opened it with a clattering of bells.

"Hey Delta. Hi Preston. There's still tea in the pot, if you'd like some."

"I'd murder a cup of tea," Preston said, hopping off Delta's shoulder and onto the front counter. Rhiannon chose that moment to walk back out to the front of the store. She narrowed her eyes at the gnome sitting on what she clearly thought was her domain.

::His boots are dirty,:: she thought, then started up meowing in protest.

"Oh, Rhiannon, Preston's fine. You have to get over yourself and share."

::I don't see why I have to share with the likes of a gnome.::

"Hey!" Preston objected. "I've been nothing but polite to you."

I rolled my eyes, because that wasn't strictly true. The cat and the gnome had been known to work together on occasion, but also tended to snipe at each other as if they were siblings, which was kind of funny if you weren't in the middle of it.

"Let me grab a couple of mugs," I said, and headed to the back again. Delta followed.

"Sarah, I really need to talk to you."

"I figured as much," I said mildly. "What about?"

I opened the cupboard and got out a mug. The tea was a little dark in the pot by now, but Delta would just have to deal.

"You know where the milk and sugar are," I said.

She sniffed, clearly used to me waiting on her. But I was over that too. I'm all about hospitality, but when people started hanging out more and more often, expecting things, I started expecting them to treat themselves as if they're at home. It's easier that way.

She doctored her tea and stirred the sweet, milky goodness, took a sip, grimaced, and added a little more sugar.

"I don't see how you're grimacing at tea when you're a coffee drinker," I replied.

She shrugged, then looked at me expectantly.

"A mug for Preston?" she asked.

"Oh, right." I got out a child-sized mug I'd recently taken from stock and put in the kitchen. It was a Peter Rabbit cup leftover from the holidays, when I had gotten in some literary-themed kitchen wares. They sold pretty well for gifts, but not so much on a regular basis.

She fixed Preston's mug too.

"Can we go back up front? I want him to hear this."

"Sure." I topped up my own mug and added a bit more cream.

Finally, we settled in around the counter, including Rhiannon, who sat at the opposite end of the long slab from the gnome. Delta glanced down at the books.

"Werewolves, vampires, and *Bunnicula*?" She raised an eyebrow and gestured with her mug. "What's going on?"

I held up a hand, "First of all, *you* came to see *me*, insisting you had something to talk to me about, which is fine. But second of all..." I looked at the books, then looked from the witch, to the cat, to the gnome. "Rhiannon says she saw a wererabbit outside last night."

"A wererabbit?" Preston exclaimed. "How big?"

::Big.::

"Well, that's exciting," Preston said, flapping his arms.

"Exciting why?" I asked. It sounded terrible to me.

"There have long been legends of the wererabbits of Seashell Cove," the gnome intoned.

"Really? I've never heard of them before," I said.

Delta looked at me and shook her head. "You still have so much left to learn, Sarah. I don't want to speak ill of your parents, but I can certainly speak ill of that uncle of yours. They should have given you a better education."

"Who are you speaking of, Delta?" It was Uncle Cyrus, doing that warlock trick of popping in again. Walking down the central bookcase aisle, he looked dapper as always. Today's outfit was black jeans, navy blue Italian shoes, and a navy striped shirt.

"You," Delta said, "Why didn't you teach her about wererabbits?"

Uncle Cyrus actually looked confused for a moment, and ran a hand across the smooth dome of his head. "Why would Sarah need to know about wererabbits?"

::Because there was one outside last night,:: Rhiannon chimed in. She looked a little too smug.

"Oh no," Uncle Cyrus groaned. "I really hope that is not true. Because if it is? This case is getting worse and worse."

19

The bells on the shop door clanged, and in came Tracy and Tabitha, each staggering under the weight of a box.

"We got the goods," Tracy said. "Hey Uncle Cyrus. Nice to see you!"

Both of the teenagers had taken to calling him uncle, because I did.

"Your sphere of influence is growing," I commented. He just raised an eyebrow at me, enigmatic as always.

"What goods?" Preston asked, hopping from foot to foot as Rhiannon batted at the tip of his bright purple cap. The gnome didn't seem to notice. The teens plunked the boxes down on the long counter.

"T-shirts," Tabitha said. She was mildly subdued. Probably afraid I was going to bring up her parents in front of everyone.

"And the notebooks!" Tracy exclaimed, rummaging around until she successfully found the box cutter. She carefully slit open both boxes, and the teens proudly withdrew....sure enough, T-shirts and notebooks. The shirts were black with a white print of a cute ghost holding a stack of books. *The Widening Gyre* was written in fancy text beneath image and the ghost had a speech bubble near its cartoon mouth that said, "Hi, I'm Biff."

Delta clapped her hands. "Those T-shirts are marvelous! Do they come in any other colors?"

Tabitha finally grinned. "Cool, right? This first round is black, but we have white on order, and wanted to ask you what other colors you might want."

"And look at these notebooks and journals! Aren't they awesome?" Tracy asked.

Some of them had the same cartoon ghost artwork, but others of them...

"These are amazing," I said. "Where did you get these photos?"

Printed on the books were photos of The Widening Gyre bookshop from the 1960s and 70s. And one of Biff alive, circa mid-1990s.

"We found a book tucked away in the back of the storage room," Tabitha said. "It's full of cool pictures."

The storage space was a walk-in closet filled with things that I hadn't gotten around to yet.

"I had no idea those were even in there." I ran my thumb across the photo of Biff on a hardcover journal. "I want this one for myself."

"We can always make more," Tabitha said, grinning ear to ear. For a Goth Wiccan, she sure was cheerful. Perky optimism was part of the charm both teens held. I was glad to see she'd relaxed again, but clearly I needed to have a private conversation with her about her parents and the fact that I wouldn't share her secrets without her permission.

It must be hard, having to hide such a major part of your life.

"Nice work, girls," Uncle Cyrus said. They both preened a bit at that.

"I know. Pretty cool, right?" Tracy said.

"I think they're clutch," Tabitha replied. I had no idea what that even meant, but from the tone of her voice, I assumed it was good.

There was definitely something about that old picture of Biff. I found it moving, as though I was all of a sudden connected to history in real time. Not only to the ghost, and the shop, and Seashell Cove, but to my history as a witch. As a psychic. As the daughter of two witches and the niece of a warlock.

I could feel the magic reaching all the way back. I felt the shop stretch and relax around me. Settling in, as if it had been waiting. Waiting for me.

And then I realized, it might not be a witch or a warlock, or anything else like it, but there was magic in the store itself. There was magic in the shelves of books.

It was so obvious. Of course books were magic. It was something I knew as a child, but had slowly forgotten, when books became a business.

I looked at the teens, tears in my eyes. "Thank you for this. It means a lot."

They blinked back at me.

"Sure. Of course," Tabitha said gently, as if I were a skittish animal.

I knew both of the girls had to be surprised. Since I

had fought them on both advertising Biff's presence and on the products.

"Thanks for sticking with things and changing my mind." I smiled and brought them both in for a hug.

Delta cleared her throat. "This is all very nice. But we need to get back to the wererabbit."

"Wererabbit?" Tabitha said. "There's wererabbits?"

Both the teens shared that excited, *Oh boy, we get to do more research,* look.

Wow. I was such a different kind of nerd when I was their age. But, to each their own.

"Yes!" Preston jumped up and down, "wererabbits."

::*Yes,*:: Rhiannon said, glaring. ::*That's what I've been trying to tell everybody, but no one listens to me. That rabbit was unnatural.*::

I cleared my throat. "Unnatural, like a talking cat?"

She huffed, jumped off the counter, and leapt back up into the front window, ears and tail twitching. I could tell she was still listening in, otherwise she would have headed to the back of the store.

"Hey," I said, "do either of you know of any new teenagers in town? Not tourists but locals who just moved here?"

Tracy shrugged. "Yeah, I've seen a couple. I mean there's that kid Ash that we said we'd look out for. We finally ran into him at the ice cream shop. He's a little freaky, quite frankly..."

Well, if Tabitha and Tracy were saying he was freaky, that meant something. Because they were into freaky things.

"No, I'm talking about two teenagers. I think they're

brothers. One of them wears a creepy Donnie Darko back patch."

"Oh them. Yeah, we've seen them a couple times, down at the beach, where the river meets the ocean," Tracy said.

"And at the Vargas's tamale parlor." Tabitha tilted her head, thinking. "I've seen them hanging out outside Tetris's shop, too."

I nodded. "That's where I saw them. But you haven't met them yet?"

"No." Tabitha grunted. "Why? Anything in particular you need to know?"

I shook my head no. "Just with everything going on, I want to keep tabs on anything new."

"The Donnie Darko patch does kinda point to an association with a wererabbit, don't you think?" Tabitha asked.

Uncle Cyrus raised his hands in frustration. "I hate that film, and I hate wereanimals!"

Huh. That was new information. It was my turn to arch an eyebrow. I was getting better at it after hours of practicing in front of my bathroom mirror.

"And why is that, exactly?"

"Yeah," said Tracy. "I mean, my mom showed us that movie last year and I thought it was brilliant."

Cyrus sighed, paced to the front display window, and looked out past the books. Was he looking for customers? Rhiannon perked up and butted his hand with her head. He scratched behind her ears, absent-mindedly.

That was also strange. Cyrus and Rhiannon were usually at a stalemate.

::He hates wererabbits because they're foolish, vicious, and small. And they chew through cables. On purpose.::

Cyrus turned back. "The cat is right. Wererabbits have a devious consciousness ticking inside their little skulls. Unscrupulous magic users often employ them for destructive purposes. I've seen more than one magical organization's computer network taken down by the beasts."

Tabitha tsked. "Isn't that wrong, painting all wererabbits with the same brush? I mean, we don't like it when people do that about us, right? Profiling?"

Cyrus grimaced, but gave the teen a respectful nod. "Perhaps you are correct. Perhaps the only wererabbits I have encountered are of the devious, vicious variety."

"Or maybe whatever turns an ordinary rabbit into a wereanimal changes their psyche in bad ways...." Tracy drummed her fingers on the opened box of notebooks.

Then she picked up *Bunnicula.* "I think it's time for a reread of this old classic. I mean, I know it's about a vampire rabbit, but there might be some clues. Don't you think?"

"Might as well," I said, shrugging noncommittally.

I didn't tell her that I'd slipped that book from the shelf because it was the only thing I thought might offer a clue.

20

My dreams that night were strange. A full, Technicolor, avant-garde movie, like one of those weird German films from the 1960s Uncle Cyrus is so fond of. But without sound.

I woke up disgruntled with strange images of rabbits with sharp teeth hopping around my back garden. The missing athame, plates, and chalices spinning through the air as if waved by an ethereal hand. Rhiannon, blinking at me, trying to communicate something. The Donnie Darko rabbit, leering down at me. A ruby ring.

Uncle Cyrus, pleading, trapped somewhere.

"Gah!" My head felt stuffed with cotton wool. I rolled out of bed and stumbled to the bathroom to splash cold water on my face before staggering to the kitchen to fill the kettle for tea.

Leaning against the quartz countertop, I texted Cyrus. I'd just seen him at the shop, and we'd had a quick meeting after work before going our separate ways, so I figured he was okay and it was just my subconscious sending out an alarm about something else. You know, the way brains do when you're sleeping. But I also knew that if I didn't check, I wouldn't be able to concentrate on anything else all day.

The image of him trapped and upset was one of the most disturbing things I'd ever seen.

It wasn't right. And I needed to make it right, somehow.

"Come on, Uncle Cyrus," I muttered to the kitchen kettle. "I need you to reply."

He didn't. But a strange pinging noise began signaling from my bedroom.

I groaned. That meant only one thing. My mother's crystal ball was trying to get my attention.

Tea would have to wait. I ran back into my bedroom, and sure enough, there on my dresser, the wooden box that housed the crystal was shaking. I opened it, and drew out the smooth crystal orb filled with striations and occlusions. My mother's crystal ball.

It was the only connection I still had with her. I wasn't sure if part of my mother's spirit was embedded in the ball—trapping her there, which was a horrifying thought—or if it was just residual magic left over from the fact that she had used the tool for decades.

At any rate, I needed to be present to the crystal now and figure out what it wanted, while I hoped against hope that Uncle Cyrus would really pop in to my kitchen any minute.

I set the ball on its little silver stand, sat on the edge of my bed, and slowed my breathing down. I needed to find my center and open my psychic senses, otherwise

—I knew from long experience—I would get nothing from the crystal. No matter how insistent its ringing was.

Making sure my feet were flat on the floor, and resting my hands on my thighs, I inhaled slowly through my nose, then slowly out through my mouth. I flexed my fingers and my toes, shrugged my shoulders and dropped them, willing myself to relax and to just breathe and be.

"Hecate, Queen of Magic... If you're out there, please come 'round. You who hold both lock and key, help me solve the mystery. Help me see what must be found, as I do will, so mote it be."

What can I say? Every witch knows that rhyming helps the magic. Whether rhyming trains the subconscious to tune in more clearly or actually does some woo-woo connecting with the cosmos or the ætheric planes thing, I can't tell you. But I rhymed anyway, and the longer I practiced, the more natural it became.

I took in one more deep, full body breath, softened my gaze, and looked into the ball. A shaft of morning sunlight from the window illuminated the surface of the crystal, but I wanted to look beyond that, into the depths, into whatever was hiding in my subconscious, or into whatever magic was hidden in the ball itself.

After what felt like forever, but was probably only three minutes of breathing and paying attention, that same swirl of dream images appeared in front of my eyes

Impatiently, I passed my hand across the ball, trying to clear the visions.

"Show me what I need to know. If I'm on the right track, shimmer and glow."

Okay, that wasn't the best rhyme in the world, but I'm a witch, not a poet.

And there it was. The image I was hoping against hope to not see.

My Uncle Cyrus, collar ripped, stubble on the usually completely smooth dome of his head. His dark eyes, boring into mine, as if trying to tell me something important.

"Where are you?" I whispered.

Magic, his image mouthed. *Trouble.*

"Magic where?" I asked, and then the vision shifted. I saw Elias Fuller's framed Masonic apron, hanging from the wall.

The image cut back to Uncle Cyrus. I could see now that he was in what looked like a small wooden room.

"Are you trapped in a closet?" I asked. "How did you get there? What happened?"

He just shook his head, looking sad.

I'm sorry, he mouthed. And then the ball clouded over, and Cyrus was gone.

"What in Hecate's name is going on?" I said to the now inert crystal ball.

Then I shook myself. There were protocols to observe. Placing both my hands lightly on the surface of the crystal, I sent a thought of thanks to whatever spirit resided there. Then I carefully wiped the surface of the ball with a soft cloth and gently nestled both it and the stand back inside the box.

Next thing on the list? I needed to gather a posse.

But first, I really really needed that tea. In a go-cup.

21

Tabitha, Tracy, and Carol were already at Angie's Cafe when I arrived, and they waved from a set of pushed-together tables in the library area near the back of the place. Good. We'd have a little more privacy there, away from the windows and the bustle of the main part of the café.

Tetris and Bart crowded in the door behind me. The aging punk and the potter must have both been watching from their shops to see when I would arrive.

"Hey, Sarah. I have to open in thirty; hope this won't take long," Bart said.

"Leave when you have to. And thanks for coming."

I had sent out a text alert to everyone I could think of, including Jerry Hamamoto. I told him to bring Ash.

I didn't fully trust the psychic yet, but Uncle Cyrus had thought that they were innocent....

Yeah, I was gonna keep a close eye on them still, but my witchy senses told me I was going to need the tarot witch's help.

I wished I had a way to contact Ah Lam Wu. As I'd driven over, I'd sent a thought into the aethers, focusing on her face, on her eyes, trying to tune in to her magical signature.

Hopefully she would hear, and respond, but I had no idea if that would work. It worked for Cyrus, but I had known him my whole life.

I left Bart and Tetris in line and threaded my way toward the back corner, where two blond heads and one black were busy conferring.

"Hey," I said, pulling out a chair. "Thanks for getting all of this set up."

"Not a problem," Tracy said, bouncing a bit in her chair. Tabitha looked a bit tired, which made me wonder if she stayed up late for parent-teen bonding time.

Angie brought over a cup of English breakfast and a Morning Glory muffin.

"You look like you could use the sustenance," she said. "It's on the house since you're helping get to the bottom of these thefts."

"Thanks, Angie," I said, "Can you stay?"

She shook her head. "No. As you can see, we're pretty busy. Morning rush."

"Yeah, sorry about taking up so much space. It was just the quickest, easiest place to get people to meet."

"No worries. Everyone's bought something, and that's all I care about, right? The bottom line."

She gave me a rueful smile and hurried off to help the people standing in line at the counter just as Delta Crabbit scurried in, banging her canvas tote bag along.

At least Rhiannon had convinced her to add a

pillow in there for Preston the gnome. After her one ride in the tote bag, the cat had deemed it uncomfortable, and therefore an unacceptable mode of transport.

Preston had agreed.

Jerry Hamamoto and Ash walked in. Ash gave a shy wave to the teenagers, who smiled back at him.

They joined the line at the counter. Then Cecilia burst in and rushed over, fuchsia hair flying, boots thumping across the wooden floors.

"Is Cyrus all right?" she asked, enfolding me in a hug smelling of motor oil and cookies.

"I don't know," I said, squeezing her arm. "But thanks for coming."

She released me and gave me a kiss on the cheek, then dropped her messenger bag on a chair across from me and headed toward the coffee line.

It felt good, having this many people to call on in my time of need. I hadn't felt this well loved since my parents were alive.

The only person who wasn't here was Stefon, who was on a client deadline. He said he would come as soon as he could, or would catch up with me later. I know a person has to make a living, but magic was taking more and more precedence over that, wasn't it? Luckily, The Widening Gyre had never done better. At least, not since Dad died.

Thank all the Gods and Goddesses for Duncan. Without him, I'd be sunk. And thank Hecate herself that the teenagers had found a way to bring more income into the shop, too.

It truly did take a village, and I was grateful for every single person in it.

Bart, Tetris, Ash, and Jerry Hamamoto sat down with their food and drinks.

"What's happening?" Jerry asked. "Your message just said it was an emergency."

He looked a bit tentative, as if picking up on the fact that I still didn't trust him. That was a good thing. I didn't want the new witch getting too comfortable before he was thoroughly checked out.

"Well," I said, taking a fortifying sip of tea, "I had bad dreams last night. Uncle Cyrus was trapped…"

"Trapped?"

"Someone stole your uncle?"

Tracy and Tabitha spoke on top of each other, stricken looks on both their faces. Carol went white as a sheet. And she hadn't started off looking so great in the first place.

All of them had grown quite fond of my uncle. I couldn't blame them. I was fond of him myself, even if I'd been a little annoyed with him lately.

I felt a pang of conscience about that. If he wasn't okay…

"Well, don't think that way." Delta grabbed my hand. "A witch's thoughts have power, you know."

"How did you know what I was thinking?" I asked.

She gave me one of those *What am I a fool?* looks. "A, it was written all over your face, and B, I am a witch."

"You were broadcasting pretty loudly," Jerry said.

Great. The new witch could read me like a book. Just what I needed. But I made a note to practice my poker face. To avoid further scrutiny, I did my best to wipe my mind and took a giant bite of the Morning

Glory muffin, enjoying the combination of carrots, raisins, and nuts.

That was another thing I did when I was stressed.

Eat.

Besides which, I had skipped breakfast. A witch needs fortification.

"What else can you tell us?" Cecilia asked, setting down a cup of black coffee and a chocolate muffin that smelled divine. The fuchsia hair framing her narrow face looked super bright. Must be freshly dyed.

"After I woke up, I consulted with mom's crystal ball and saw him again. He was in a small wood room, like a closet. I think he's at the Fuller Mansion."

Everyone stared at me for a moment.

"Do you think this is related to the thefts?" Bart asked.

"I don't see how, but they have to be, right? Someone wants this collection of objects for some reason, and there is a link to that mansion. You know, because Elias Fuller's ring is missing, too."

I didn't tell them that there was already a full-scale investigation into the ring, and that Uncle Cyrus had been part of that. The teens and Stefon knew, of course, which meant Carol did, too. But to the rest of the people at the table? I didn't feel right sharing my uncle's magical business. Heck, he barely told me about it half the time.

I also didn't feel up to explaining that something was up between Elias Fuller and Bunny, and that Bunny was keeping a secret. It was probably nothing more than the ghost flapper heightening the drama of being jilted.

"...think I should do a reading about this," Jerry was saying.

"I think you're right," Delta replied.

"You're gonna do it here, Dad?" Ash squirmed in his chair, looking super uncomfortable. "I thought you said we didn't do those kinds of things in public."

Jerry ruffled Ash's spiky hair. Ash ducked. Tabitha and Tracy smiled in sympathy.

"Usually, that's true," Jerry said. "But sometimes, needs must, kid."

Ash looked down and shook his head. Was it just tween embarrassment, or something else?

Jerry pulled a small, rectangular velvet sack from a backpack on the floor. The sack was purple, and embroidered with stars and moons in shades of silver and green. From the sack, he withdrew a battered Tarot deck with foxed edges and set it on the table in front of him.

"I want everybody to hold the deck, and think of Sarah's uncle, Cyrus."

I felt a pang of uncertainty, and my two cups of tea soured a bit in my stomach. First of all, we were acting as if Cyrus was dead or something, and I didn't like it. Second of all, I still felt uneasy with Jerry Hamamoto and his magic. I just didn't know enough about him yet.

"Hey, it's okay, babe." Stefon's warm rumble of a voice came from behind me. I hadn't even noticed him walk into the café. He kissed the top of my head and pulled over another chair.

The teens and Delta scooted over to give him more room.

"I'm not sure how this is going to help anything,"

Carol said.

Tracy's mother looked really stressed, as if she hadn't been sleeping well. And she was still way too pale. If someone had stolen my ritual knife, I would probably look the same.

"Are you one hundred percent sure your uncle is missing?" she asked.

I shook my head. "I don't know. But I had this weird dream and saw the vision in the crystal ball. Plus, I texted him this morning and sent out a psychic call. I sent one to his colleague, too. We'll see if anyone responds, but I wanted to get ahead of this, and not wait for confirmation. If something really is wrong, we need to be able to move fast."

As I was speaking, the cards were making their way around the table, finally reaching me. I held the deck lightly between both palms.

Huh. They felt good. There wasn't a bad signature about them, so that was slightly reassuring.

I breathed in deeply. Closed my eyes. Then I thought of Uncle Cyrus. Of his beautiful clothes, his frankincense and Bay Rum perfume, and how much I loved him.

I got a little teary eyed, at that. He really did mean the world to me, especially now that both my parents were gone.

Uncle Cyrus, I thought. *I hope you're safe.*

And I hoped he was once again just busy working on something, and my subconscious was freaking out about it.

But if you are trapped, we're going to come get you. We'll figure it out.

22

———————

I passed the cards along.

They slowly made their way back to Jerry Hamamoto, who set them out in a standard Celtic cross.

Usually, I loved watching other witches work, but I couldn't really focus on the cards. I was too upset.

So I exhaled, shoved more muffin into my mouth, and took a sip of tea. Then I leaned into Stefon, needing as much comfort as possible. As I settled in, I noticed the clown at the counter. Guess even clowns needed caffeine.

My knight in geeky T-shirt and jeans grabbed my left hand in his large mitt and kissed my knuckles. I could feel the calluses on palms and fingers from hefting his sword and lifting weights. There were also calluses on his fingertips, from hours of video gaming and programming.

I focused on our clasped fingers resting on the tabletop, as I listened to Jerry Hamamoto speak.

"There are a lot of major arcana cards here, which lends weight to the reading, and usually offers more clarity.... But I'm also getting a sense of confusion from the cards. Especially this one. The seven of cups."

I looked up at that, to see him tap a finger against a card showing a dark figure standing before a cloud. Floating on the clouds were cups holding a variety of strange objects. Jewels. Castles. Serpents... Clearly tuning in to the cards, Jerry's eyes never left the images arrayed in front of him.

It was the classic deck, designed by Pamela Coleman Smith, showing a variety of characters in medieval clothing.

"You recognize those outfits?" I murmured to Stefon.

"Babe. I'm trying to listen."

Right. Bad witch. Taking a hefty sip of now-tepid tea, I grimaced and turned my attention back to the reading. Just because I was freaking out was no reason not to take in all the information I could.

"What's the main source of confusion?" Carol asked.

Jerry looked down at the cards, then glanced at me, then back at the cards.

As if he didn't want to hold my gaze.

"I... don't really..."

Preston smacked a tiny hand on the table, purple cap bobbing. "Just spit it out, witch!"

Jerry swallowed.

"Preston!" Delta hissed, then shoved the gnome back down into the tote bag on her lap.

The clown peered back at our table, go-cup in

hand. So did some other folks. I guess everyone had heard the gnome. Just great. We were no longer incognito.

"I'm afraid that the cards point to you," he finally said.

I looked around the table, trying to figure out who he was talking about. Then I got it.

Every single person at the table—human, witch, and one disgruntled-looking gnome—was looking right at me.

There was complete silence at the table, which made the café noises even louder. Laughter. The hiss of the milk steamer. The nineties playlist Angie favored.

"Well," Delta Crabbit said, glaring at Jerry.

"You better have something good to back that up," Cecilia chimed in. She looked as if Jerry had betrayed her best friend. Right. That would be me. I swallowed a lump of gratitude, then flared with annoyance.

"I have no idea what you're talking about. How is the confusion around me?"

"Your dreams," Delta said. "How accurate are they, usually?"

"I... I don't know."

But between Delta's question and the reading, I was now doubting everything. Was that Jerry Hamamoto's intention? To sow the seeds of self doubt inside me and everyone around me, taking suspicion off of himself and his son?

I didn't have too much time to think on it, before there was a flurry of activity at the front of the café.

The two teenage boys shoved their way toward our

table in the back. They looked frantic, both of their tan faces flushed with red, sandy-brown hair a mess.

"Are you the witch?" said the older one in the sleeveless jean jacket.

"I don't know about *the* witch," I said, glancing around the table, "but..."

"But you're the one who fixes things, right?" asked the younger boy. Around twelve or thirteen, he had one snaggle tooth and a dusting of freckles across his nose.

"What do you need?" Stefon interjected. Thank Hecate.

"Our rabbit is missing."

"Yeah," said the older boy. "And we heard you were good at finding stuff."

"Well, not lately," I muttered. But this was pretty serious—a live animal missing is quite different from just a bunch of missing objects.

"Wait," said Tabitha. "You have the wererabbit?"

"Wererabbit?" said the younger boy, wrinkling his nose in confusion. Kind of like a rabbit, now that I thought of it. "No, it was just a plain old rabbit."

"At least we think so." The older brother's face paled beneath his tan.

"Huh," said Tabitha. "Who are you anyway?"

"Yeah," Tracy chimed in, "you just burst in on our private meeting without introducing yourselves."

The teens squared off, all of them looking defensive.

"Hey," I said, raising a hand. "It's all right. They're just upset. Right?"

The boys both nodded mutely.

"But can you help us?" asked the younger one, brown eyes pleading.

Gah. I hate it when young people plead with me like that. I'm such a sucker.

"I can try, but I can't make you any promises. We have a lot going on here."

"But it's our rabbit." The younger teen's lower lip quivered. I swear it did.

Double ugh. I looked around the table.

"Anyone have any ideas?" Everyone shrugged or shook their heads.

"Okay," I said. "Anything else from you?"

I looked at Jerry Hamamoto, who held my eyes with his. After way too long, he said, "I think there's still more here, but I'm going to need to sit with it. See if any more messages come through."

"All right." Well, this whole meeting had felt like a bust, and the tarot reading was worse than useless. I felt more confused than ever, and clearly that had influenced the cards. "Sorry I brought you all here. I had hoped we could pool some information. But, let's all go our separate ways and keep working on it. Okay? But keep checking your phones."

"We trust you, Sarah," Tetris said. "But I have to get to work anyway."

"Okay, thanks for coming. You too, Bart."

Both shop owners hurried out.

Cecilia gave me a hug. I was so grateful my ex-girlfriend was now my best friend.

"If it turns out you need help rescuing Cyrus, Raul and I are on board. He wanted me to tell you that. Toby, too, if you need them."

"Thanks, Cecilia. And tell the others thank you, too. I'll text you later."

I looked around at the half cleared table. I should be getting to the store, too.

"Anyone else who wants to, come with me to the store, including you two," I said to the boys. "I need to check in with Rhiannon."

"Who's Rhiannon?" the older boy whispered to Tracy.

She looked smug. "The witch's cat."

"Wow," said the younger one. "Cool."

"Okay, let's clear up so we don't leave a mess for Angie. Put the tables back..."

"I'll take care of that, babe," Stefon said. "You go on ahead. I'll meet you there in a couple of minutes."

"Thanks Stefon," I gave him a light kiss. "You really are the best."

He grinned. "I know."

23

———

"Thanks for opening, Duncan."

"No problem, boss."

Today, Duncan was wearing a kind-of-sort-of-Hawaiian-style black and white shirt with dancing skeletons all over it.

His heavy, black-rimmed glasses were a stark contrast to his pale face and the currently bleached white-blond hair sticking up like dandelion fluff around his head. He was a cutie, that Duncan. But then I feel that way about everyone I like, don't I?

"Hey Duncan!" Tracy said, bouncing into the store. The two brothers followed, looking much more subdued. I still hadn't figured out their names.

"You around today?" Duncan asked me.

"I hope so. But we may need to head to Portland again. How were things with Delta?"

"She was great. It all worked out fine. We made a lot of sales, but weren't so busy that we couldn't handle it."

Well, that was a relief.

"Is there trouble?" Duncan asked, brow furrowing.

"You know..." I sighed. "There always seems to be trouble lately. But yeah, I think something might be wrong with Uncle Cyrus. I haven't heard from him since yesterday."

Duncan started rooting around in a stack of papers next to the cash point on the counter.

"Oh, speaking of which, someone came and knocked on the door this morning before I opened. Friend of his. A hot older woman. Asian. What was her name...?"

He ruffled through more papers.

"Ah Lam Wu?" I asked.

"Oh! Yes, that was it. I told her you were probably down at Angie's, but she didn't want to intrude. Said she come back later."

Had Ah Lam answered my summons? I hoped so, because if she was in town on her own, it probably meant something really was wrong with Uncle Cyrus. Just great.

"Well, I need to have a meeting with these two." I jerked a thumb toward the brothers. "Hopefully, she'll come back and I'll find out what she wants."

"All right." I turned back to the boys. "First of all, what are your names? I'm Sarah, by the way, and this is Tracy and Tabitha."

"Hi," said the younger one, scuffing a worn sneaker on the wood floor. "I'm Colin. And this is my older brother, Roger."

"Good to meet you. Come on back."

I lead the boys down the aisle through the bookcases.

"And hello, Rhiannon," I said out loud. "You can make an appearance at any time now."

"Is her cat invisible?" Colin whispered.

"No," Tabitha replied. I could almost hear the eye roll. "Cats just do what they want. And they're good at hiding."

"Right," Colin said, as if she had imparted some great wisdom.

And sure enough, Rhiannon slinked around the edge of a bookcase and paused to stretch. She had clearly been taking a nap.

She also had a wicked gleam in her eye. That made me suspicious.

"Rhiannon? Remember that rabbit you were telling us about?" I swear she shrugged, though how it is possible for a cat to shrug, I don't know.

"You can talk to your cat," Colin said.

"Everyone talks to their cat, silly." That was Tracy this time. It was clear the two slightly older girls were feeling superior to poor young Colin. And silent Roger, who I now noticed had the creepy Donnie Darko patch on his back. He hadn't said a word.

::*What do these two have to do with the rabbit?*:: Rhiannon asked.

"They say it's their rabbit. And it's missing."

"When did it go missing?" Tabitha asked Colin.

"Two nights ago."

"That's when you said you saw the rabbit, right?" I stared down at the black cat, who glared back at me.

::*Yes. That's exactly what I told you, if you would only pay attention.*"

"Give me a break," I muttered.

"What's she's saying?" Colin asked.

Tabitha answered. "She's saying she saw your rabbit outside the shop. She told us it was wererabbit."

Rhiannon sneezed.

"You were pulling our legs, weren't you, with all that Bunnicula stuff, right?" Tracy asked, arms crossed over her Biff the Book Ghost T-shirt.

Rhiannon washed one black paw.

Finally, Roger spoke. "Wasn't Bunnicula a vampire rabbit, not a wererabbit?"

"Don't go splitting hairs on me," I said, "no pun intended. We're trying to get to the bottom of this and I can't help you if *some* people"—I stared at Rhiannon—"keep confusing matters when we're in the middle of a case."

Colin asked, "What case? You mean there's more going on than just our missing rabbit?"

Oh no. I actually groaned. Now more people were involved, and civilians to boot. All because I wasn't thinking clearly, and had just spewed information out at random.

"That," I said firmly, "is none of your business."

"Yeah," said Tracy.

"It's private witch business," Tabitha said.

I shot both teens a look, hoping they would get the message and be quiet. We sat down in the cozy nook beneath the stained glass window. Tabitha and Tracy grabbed a couple more chairs from Biff's favorite paranormal section in the back of the shop.

"Sorry, Biff," I heard Tabitha say.

"Who's Biff?" Roger asked. "Another cat?"

"Never mind," I replied.

"Biff's a ghost," Tracy said brightly.

"You have a ghost?" Colin yelped.

Great. This was getting worse and worse. And more and more distracted and confused.

But, what was I going to do about it? Nothing.

"All right, how long have you had this rabbit?"

Both boys looked at each other, clearly communicating something they didn't want me to know.

"It is your rabbit, isn't it?" I asked.

"It's ours!" Colin burst out. "It's totally ours. We found it. It was hopping towards the beach."

"Is that right?" I asked Roger. He nodded.

"Yeah."

"Why would I lie about that?" Colin said. "We probably saved its life!"

Okay. The plot thickened. There was now a rabbit missing. Possibly a wereanimal, and who knew who it belonged to or where it had come from? I would add it to the list of missing things.

I heard the bells at the front door ring.

"Sarah," Duncan called back. "You have a visitor."

I stood, and turned to the four expectant faces looking up at me.

"All right. You two," I said to Tabitha and Tracy, "gather as much information from Colin and Roger as you possibly can. And take notes."

"Don't we always?" Tabitha asked.

I nodded. That was one thing the teens were super good at.

"Thank you. I'll be back in a minute."

I headed to the front. As I suspected, it was the

tasteful and elegant Ah Lam Wu, looking as out of place in Seashell Cove as Uncle Cyrus always did.

She didn't look quite as well put together as she had last time I saw her though. Strands of hair fell from her neat bun and there was a scuff marring one of her shoes.

"Ms. Wu."

"Please," she said, "call me Ah Lam."

"Is everything all right?" I asked.

"I'm afraid not," she said. "Your uncle has been abducted."

The room swam in front of my eyes. I reached out to grab the counter.

"Breathe, Sarah," Duncan said. "Here, have a seat."

He dragged me behind the counter and helped me onto the stool.

I lowered my head into my hands and took in three deep breaths. My heart raced like an Olympic runner's. I looked up at Ms. Wu, who gazed at me with great concern.

"I was hoping it wasn't true," I said. "And the tarot reader said I was confused...."

"Tell me what you know," she replied.

I shook my head, trying to clear it. Duncan brought me a cup of water.

"Thanks, Duncan." I drank the whole thing down before replying.

"I had bad dreams last night. Cyrus was trapped. And then I consulted my mother's crystal ball—actually, it alerted me—and I saw him in a wooden room."

All the images came tumbling back in. My mouth tasted sour with fear.

"He was clearly trapped and didn't look well. I assume he's at the Fuller Mansion somewhere?"

Ah Lam nodded. "There are multiple hidden passageways and rooms in that place. But I haven't been able to get any of them open."

I sat up straight and shoved the empty glass away. "Well, he's not going to stay hidden or trapped for long. Not if I have anything to do with it. And I don't care how old and historic that mansion is, I just happen to have a boyfriend with an ax."

Ah Lam Wu's eyes widened. But she didn't say no.

24

———

Ms. Wu and I began formulating a plan. Or really, she did. The only idea I had so far was enlisting Stefon and his ax to hack through walls, and maybe siccing Cecilia, Raul, and their crew on whoever it was who was doing this to Uncle Cyrus.

The bells on the shop door rang, and in walked a customer. Just great. Usually I welcomed customers with open arms. But right now, I just didn't have time. Plus, I didn't want anyone else in the crossfire. Standing just inside the doorway was a tall, skinny white man with pale blue eyes and nondescript brown hair. He wore a white T-shirt, black pants, and black sneakers with a red stripe. In his arms, he carried a massive gray and white rabbit. I mean, the thing was seriously huge.

"Rhiannon, you were not exaggerating," I murmured.

"Chuckles!" Colin said, and ran towards the man, who leaned his whole torso away, clutching at the rabbit who began kicking to get down. Rhiannon darted towards the man and hissed, swiping at his legs.

"Ouch!" he shouted, dancing on one foot. "Get that creature away from me!"

"Wait a minute, Chuckles," I said, "I know who you are."

"You're the creepy clown," Tracy said.

"I'm not creepy, I'm just trying to make an honest living. And my name is not Chuckles!"

"Is that why you stole our rabbit?" Roger sputtered, his tanned face red with anger.

Whoa, that was a surprise. Donnie Darko had fangs.

"You stole Chuckles!" Roger said, voice filled with menace.

Oh. So the rabbit was Chuckles? Okay.

Stefon chose that moment to walk into the store. It took him about two seconds to assess the situation and stand, arms crossed over his broad chest, bulky frame blocking the exit.

The clown's eyes darted back and forth from Stefon, to me, to the teens, to the brothers, and then to Ah Lam Wu.

When he saw her, he grew even paler. Well now, that was interesting. Clearly, he recognized her power.

"Who are you?" I asked. "And what are you doing with that rabbit?"

"It's my rabbit. These two stole Eva from me."

"Eva," I said.

"Yes. You think Chuckles is a better name?" He actually looked offended. I couldn't blame him. The rabbit kicked some more. The clown struggled to keep a grip on her.

"Look at her!" Colin said. "She doesn't like you. Let her go!"

The man squeezed the rabbit tighter. She really did look uncomfortable, and I swear the thing had to weigh fifteen pounds. I'd never seen a rabbit that big.

"So, I have to ask. Is that a wererabbit?"

"What, are you nuts, lady? Of course not. Eva's a magician's rabbit, but she ran away."

"Well," I said, "quite frankly, I can see why. You don't seem like you treat her very well."

He sniffed. "She gets food and water. And she has a job. What more can a rabbit want?"

"Love," Colin said. "We love her. We were taking good care of her until you stole her."

"I reclaimed her. Reclaimed my property."

"She's not property," Roger said, inching closer, "she's her own being."

Here we were again, arguing about the personhood of a possibly magical animal. This was my life now. Figuring out personhood is more complex than you might think. Turns out, pretty much everything has some kind of personhood, if you look at it long enough.

Ah Lam Wu stepped closer. The clown stepped back and yelped when he bumped into Stefon.

The warlock sniffed ostentatiously. "You stink of magic. But I'm not sure what kind. The rabbit, too."

A feral grin split his white face. "Haven't figured it out, hmmm? And you're supposed to be all powerful. Just like that Cyrus thought he was so much better than me. All hoity toity. Well, look at him now."

I wanted to wipe that sneer off his face.

"What have you done with him?" I growled. Now it was my turn to step forward.

Stefon grabbed the rabbit. Strangely enough, the creature came willingly into Stefon's arms. Supporting the animal's legs, his eyes zeroed in on Colin.

"You there. Kid." Stefon held out the rabbit. Colin ran forward and grabbed her, cradling her against his chest. The man jerked toward the rabbit. Stefon clapped his hands on the man's skinny shoulders.

"Chuckles," Colin said, gazing adoringly into the rabbit's eyes. "You're okay."

Personally, I thought Eva was a better name than Chuckles. I had to agree with the creepy clown guy on that. But then, I'm not a thirteen-year-old kid.

And who knew what the rabbit's actual name was?

Now that the clown-man-magician-whatever was secured, Rhiannon paused to clean the blood off her claws.

::*She likes whatever the boys want to call her*,:: Rhiannon said. ::*And she really hates this guy. By the way, he didn't treat her well at all.*::

Well, that wasn't surprising.

"What have you done with my uncle?" I said, again. "If you have hurt him..."

"Hurt one hair on his bald head, you mean? I would never do that." He smirked. "Why don't you tell your boyfriend here to unhand me, or things are going to get nasty."

"Keep ahold of him," Ah Lam Wu said.

"Oh, he's not going anywhere," Stefon replied.

And then the air shimmered. The clown twisted

and jerked, elbows flying, busting out of Stefon's hold. He disappeared into a seam that suddenly appeared in the middle of the bookshop.

"What the heck?" Duncan said from behind me. I'd forgotten he was even there.

"What the heck?" Tabitha and Tracy shouted.

And then, before the seam could close, Ah Lam Wu looked at me.

"Sorry. I have to go. Get to the mansion as quickly as you can."

She leapt through the shimmering seam, which closed with a snap. Stefon yelped, as if it burned his fingers. Then he looked at me, dark eyes wide with shock.

"You know I love you, right?"

I nodded, feeling as shocked as he looked. I'm sure my eyes were as big as saucers.

"Like really," he said, shaking off his hands and moving toward me. "I love you. But since hooking up with you? My life has gotten seriously weird."

He pressed a light kiss to my forehead and embraced me as if I were a lifeline.

"What do we do now?" Tracy asked, breaking through our little moment.

Right.

"I'll contact Cecilia and Raul. And then we're all going to the Fuller Mansion, and we're getting my uncle back."

I turned to my store manager. "Sorry, Duncan. You're on your own again."

He was wiping sweat off his face with a blue bandana and looked a bit peaked.

"That's fine," he said, voice sounding shaky. "You do what you have to do. I'll mind the store."

The subtext was loud and clear: give me something normal and ordinary to do, and please leave me out of your strangeness.

I wish life was that simple and easy for all the people around me, but it wasn't. It never had been, and it probably never would be.

"Thanks, Duncan. Ping Delta if you need her," I said, then crouched down. "And Rhiannon, keep an eye on things here, too, okay?"

::On it.::

She let me scratch behind her ears for ten seconds. When I stood up, everyone was staring at me. Waiting.

"All right," I said, "anyone who needs to, hit the bathroom. Get some water. Then let's go. Tracy. Call your mother and let her know you and Tabitha are coming with me."

I knew Carol was slammed with work, or I might have asked her to come, too. Though frankly, since her athame had gone missing, I wasn't sure how much I could trust her magic. It wasn't that she needed her athame to do it, but the heart had gone out of her.

And that made her less reliable in a magical fight.

"What about us?" Colin asked.

I turned to the two brothers, who looked stunned, but determined.

"You two? Take care of that rabbit. And figure out if it's a wereanimal. Somehow."

Meanwhile, something on the front counter tugged at my psychic senses. It was the new display of reading-related necklaces set up near the fancy pens. Hanging among the dangling book charms and pendants made of famous quotes behind beveled glass was one weighted brass pendulum, leftover from our Samhain display of occult books and paraphernalia.

I lifted it from the display and tucked it into the watch pocket of my jeans, making a note to adjust inventory later.

Then I texted Cecilia, hoping against hope we weren't too late.

And that Uncle Cyrus was okay.

25

———

The Fuller Mansion was eerily quiet, except for the stream of 1920s expletives Bunny the ghost was spouting. I don't even know how she got into the car. We were already en route when Tracy started freaking out because there was a ghost in her lap. We finally got that all sorted, though it had been a long drive.

So here we were, in the ornate, Victorian vestibule. Me. Stefon, with his ax slung against one shoulder. Then there were Tracy and Tabitha, and close behind, Raul and Cecilia. Those two had not only followed us in Cecilia's classic muscle car, but brought a small toolbox that was filled with only the necessities, Cecilia said. They both insisted that if we needed to break in to a hidden closet, screwdrivers and pry bars might be more effective than a large medieval ax.

What can I say? Whatever it took to break Cyrus out, I was going to use, including the pendulum, which was not one of my usual tools. But hey, any magical tool in a storm, right?

We crept towards the library. A fire crackled deep within the large fireplace at the end of the room. Who had lit it? And wasn't it dangerous to leave a fire burning around so many books?

I looked around, and sure enough, the place was empty, as if all the ghosts were hiding.

"They here?" Stefon asked.

I shook my head. "No. The place is empty."

"Where to?" Tracy asked, bouncing nervously. Cecilia and Raul stared, gobsmacked, at the carved lintels and sumptuous rugs. The mansion really was impressive. Too bad we were here to tear the place apart.

A commotion started up from the foyer, and we ran back towards the entryway, only to see Bunny grappling with Elias Fuller on the stairs.

::*Get off me, you slattern!*::

::*How dare you?*:: she shrieked. ::*You rat!*::

Guess the honeymoon phase was already over. And if you've never had a ghost screaming inside your head, let me tell you, it's highly unpleasant.

It looked like they were wrestling over an object. I couldn't tell what until Bunny, with a look of triumphant glee on her face, flung a shining object over the rail.

::*Catch!*:: she cried, as Elias Fuller roared.

Tabitha lurched forward, arms outstretched. I heard a small smack as whatever it was hit her palm.

"Hey," she said, turning to us. "It looks like Old Granddad's watch!"

Sure enough, dangling from her fingers on a gold chain was an elaborate pocket watch. But how in the world had it gotten here?

"Elias Fuller," I said, raising my voice to carry over the ghost fight. "Have you been stealing things from Seashell Cove? And did you steal your own ring?"

"What the heck?" Stefon said. "The Mason stole his own ring?"

Yeah. That last part didn't make any sense, did it?

And my bet was still on the creepy clown.

::*I most certainly did not!*:: Fuller bellowed.

Ah Lam Wu appeared beside me. I yelped, clutching my heart.

"Give a witch some warning, why don't you?"

"Sorry," she said. "No time. What is happening here?"

"Elias Fuller and Bunny are fighting," I said, stating the obvious to anyone who could see the ghosts, still grappling on the staircase. It was truly a strange sight. A flapper and a Victorian lumber baron, grappling and yelping, fading in and out of view.

"And it looks like Elias is part of at least some of the thefts," I continued. "Though I can't quite figure out how."

"Old Granddad did say it was as if a force came out of nowhere and stole his watch, didn't he?" Tracy asked.

"That he did," I replied. I tucked the thought away, then turned back to Ah Lam. "But more importantly, did you find Cyrus?" I asked. "And where's the clown?"

Ah Lam Wu shuddered. "That clown is seriously bad news. I swear, he came out of nowhere. He was not on our radar at all." She tapped a finger against her lips. Her nail polish matched her perfect lipstick. Burgundy wine. I seriously needed to up my game.

"At least you got the rabbit from him," she said.

"Wait? The rabbit is key to this?" I said, then glanced up at Bunny and Elias. It looked like their fight was going to go on for some time, and as Bunny was getting a few good licks in. I didn't feel very compelled to stop them.

Meanwhile, we were all standing around as if my uncle wasn't still trapped inside this house somewhere. We needed to figure out a plan, and soon....

"Babe, what is going on?" Stefon asked. I kept forgetting he couldn't see ghosts.

"The two ghosts are still fighting on the steps and Ah Lam here says the rabbit is key to the clown's power somehow."

She nodded, looking grave. "He ensorcelled the rabbit, and was using it as a familiar to boost his power. My supposition is that's how the clown connected with the ghosts and started stealing things."

Forcing a creature to be your familiar went against every magical tenet and protocol. She was right, this clown really was bad news. Though how he had pulled all this off was still a mystery.

"But why?" Tracy asked.

Tabitha and Tracy had clustered next to us. Tabitha slid the watch into her front jeans pocket. Cecilia and Raul were looking around, the expressions on their faces a cross between interested and appalled.

Frankly, I was surprised Raul didn't look more freaked out.

"You doing okay, Raul?"

He nodded. "Catholic family. We're used to all kinds of strange things."

I shrugged. That was good to know.

"Babe," Stefon said, "all this is very interesting, and I'm sure the information is important as heck. But we really need to find your uncle, don't we?"

"Right," I said. "I keep getting distracted. Maybe *that's* the confusion Jerry Hamamoto picked up on in the cards, or maybe...the seven of cups card he thought was about me—and truthfully, that might be part of it. Cards can have more than one meaning—but right now? I think that card is about the clown, bamboozling us all."

"I think you're right," Ah Lam said, mouth set in a straight line. She looked pissed. It's never good to cross a warlock. It's especially not good to kidnap a warlock's colleague.

"Any clues as to where they might be in this place?" Raul asked, picking up his tool box.

Cecilia stepped forward and slipped her hand in mine, giving it a squeeze of reassurance.

"Thanks," I said. I needed that. I looked from her, to Stefon, to the teens, to Ah Lam and Raul. How'd I get so lucky, to have friends and family like this?

"Okay," I said. "Here's the plan. We're going to split up into two groups. One group starts at the top of the mansion, and the other will start here, on the ground floor. Each group needs a person who is handy with basic tools. Ah Lam? You go with one group, and I'll take the other, okay?"

"Let's do this," she said.

26

———

Tabitha and Tracy went with Ah Lam Wu, along with Raul and his toolbox. That left me with Stefon and his ax and Cecilia with a screwdriver and a wrench. I took the pendulum out of my pocket, just in case. My intuition had insisted I bring it, and a witch always listens to their intuition. It was one of the first things I learned early on. You don't listen? It stops working.

"Okay," I said, squaring my shoulders. "Let's start at the top of the house. But first..." I looked up the stairs where Bunny and Elias had stopped grappling, but were still arguing. Very loudly. At least I'd managed to tune them out. Turning them into ghostly white noise helped.

"First we have to get past those two."

Stefon shrugged and adjusted his grip on the ax.

"I can't see them, so I don't care," he said. "I'm also bigger than both of you. So why don't I lead the way? I bet they'll move when they see me coming."

I wasn't so sure about that, but it was as good of an idea as any.

"All right," Cecelia said. "Lead on, Macduff."

Stefon grinned at the mangled Shakespearean reference and headed up the carved wooden stairs. Sure enough, halfway up, I heard Bunny shriek, and heard an *oof* from Elias Fuller.

Stefon was right. He had apparently plowed right through the ghosts, sending them who knows where. All I cared about was that they weren't on the stairs by the time I got there.

At the top of the stairs was a landing. I paused to get my bearings. A long, carpeted hallway veered off in both directions.

"Which way?" Cecelia asked.

"Not sure," I said, "but let me check something."

I wrapped the chain of the pendulum around the pointer finger of my right hand, then held out my left hand, palm up. I breathed gently across the pointed weight and whispered, "Pendulum, find the giver of this gift, travel through the magic rift. Through the corridors we go, can you do this, yes or no?"

Asking yes and no questions was the one thing I had learned when Cyrus taught me how to use the pendulum. For this particular pendulum, "yes" was a clockwise circle, and a "no" sent it swinging side to side.

I held both my hands as still as possible, and inhaled slowly, paused for a moment, and then exhaled. I imagined the link between the hunk of pointed brass and my uncle and magical mentor. I saw it as a twining thread of light, linking the pendulum to his face. Not the upset face of a trapped warlock, but the face of the kind and confident person who had been part of my life since the day I was born.

"Find Uncle Cyrus," I repeated. "Can you do this? Yes, or no?"

The pendulum moved very slightly in a clockwise circular direction. Not the large sweeping circle I'd been hoping for, but hey, it was positive movement and I'd take it.

"Okay," I said, looking at my friends. "The connection is not very strong. But it says it can help."

"Better than nothing," Stefon replied.

"That's pretty cool, frankly," Cecilia said. "It really looked like it moved all on its own. I didn't know you worked with pendulums."

I looked at my friend. The black and hot pink striped jeans and black T-shirt she'd donned today matched her fuchsia hair and dark eyes.

"I don't," I said. "Not usually. But if it helps Cyrus, I will. Okay pendulum. Can you swing in the general direction we should head?"

I made my body still again, slowed my breathing down. Stefon and Cecilia also stood stock still, all three of us staring at the brass weight that hovered above my left palm.

Very slightly, there was movement, swinging toward my right.

"Looks like we're heading that way," Stefon said.

"I'm ready," Cecilia replied, brandishing the screwdriver in one hand and the wrench in the other.

"We're coming, Cyrus," I said, and started walking down the carpet runner toward a series of doors, some closed, some open. We passed a study. A bedroom. A bathroom with a claw foot tub and stained glass window.

"Anything?" Cecilia asked.

The pendulum kept gently rocking in the direction my feet were pointed.

"It's hard to tell, since I'm walking, but it feels right."

So on we went, toward a small white door with a stained glass window at the end of the hall. The longer we traversed the long hallway, the thicker the air seemed, pushing at my thighs like a force field. The pendulum's swing grew stronger, practically snapping itself horizontally, pointing toward the small white door.

"Whoa," Cecilia murmured. "That's really swinging."

I didn't answer, needing to keep myself as steady as possible, moving step by step toward the door.

"Do you want me to go through first?" Stefon asked. I knew that it was hard for him and his knightly nature to ask such a thing, rather than go barreling on ahead.

"No," I ground out. "But someone needs to open the door."

We were there, sunlight bouncing through the colored glass, reflecting on the faces of two of the most important people in my life. Now, if only we could safely rescue the third.

Cecilia snaked a small arm in front of me and turned the knob. The door creaked open, letting in a blast of air, sunshine, and birdsong, and the sound of the freeway three blocks off.

"Here goes," I said, stepping through.

The view was incredible. The whole city and the

river were spread out on all three sides of the open cupola. Carved wooden arches framed the view, unimpeded by glass. I stepped dead center in the little round outdoor room, flanked by Stefon and Cecilia.

The pendulum stopped.

I breathed, trying to feel the mansion itself. Connecting with the spirit of the building. Trying to sense Uncle Cyrus.

"He's here," I said. I felt him as I felt the blood thrumming in my veins. I felt the teens, Raul, and Ah Lam, somewhere down below.

"Where are you, Cyrus?" I whispered the words to the mounting breeze that caught at my hair and blew it across my eyes.

"Sarah?" Stefon's voice was urgent.

"What?"

"The pendulum."

It had stopped, point down toward my left palm, but a vibration began at the tip, radiating upward, tightening the chain around my finger until it dug into my skin.

"What's it doing?" Cecilia asked.

"I don't know," I said. And then I did. It swung in a great, circular arc, rising higher and higher until it carved a circle in the air. But it didn't stop. The swing continued, first larger and larger, then smaller and smaller, as the pendulum did something no pendulum should ever have a right to do.

It was pointing, tip upward, arcing tighter and tighter still.

Until it vibrated, quivering, pointing at the wooden bead board ceiling above our heads.

27

::*Whatever are you doing?*:: Elias Fuller's voice bellowed in my head.

::*Leave her alone!*:: That was Bunny. They both crashed through the open doorway and crowded into the cupola space.

::*You must cease this activity, now! You are uninvited guests in my home and I will not stand for it.*::

::*Shut your trap, you duffer!*::

"Both of you, be quiet!" I shouted, startling Stefon and Cecilia both.

"But..." Stefon stammered.

"Not you. The ghosts are here. Bunny and Elias."

I smacked my left hand around the pendulum to stop its vibrating, and unwound the chain from my right index finger. The chain had left small dents in my skin. I thanked the pendulum and tucked it safely in my pocket before turning to the apoplectic Elias Fuller.

The ghost looked scared. What had scared Elias Fuller?

Unfortunately, I didn't have time to puzzle it out. Cyrus was still trapped and a demented clown was still on the loose.

"He's up there," I said, doing my best to ignore the battling ghosts. But, dang it, their scrabbling bumped though me, spreading a chill over my left side. Gah. How was I supposed to concentrate?

"Bunny! Please! Get him out of here!" I shouted. I had no idea if she could, but I was desperate, and knew that the angry flapper would try her utmost. A lover scorned and all that.

Uncle Cyrus, I thought, *we're coming to get you.*

I turned to my boyfriend. His face was grave. One hand stroked his curly beard, the other gripped his ax. Waiting. Ready.

"What do you want us to do?" Cecilia asked. She was standing near one of the open facets of the cupola, looking around with wide eyes, wrench and screwdriver at the ready.

"I want Stefon to bust through the ceiling." Both of their eyes grew wide. "Which means you and I are going to have to back up, Cecilia."

Stefon nodded, but his lips turned down.

"You sure?" he asked.

"No," I said, "I'm not sure."

I looked up at the possibly-one-hundred-thirty-year-old white bead board and apologized to the designer and the builders of the grand place.

"I'm not sure," I said, "but it's the only way I can think of to get him free."

"Okay then," Stefon said. He rolled his shoulders, exhaled, and raised his ax.

"Nooooo!" shouted a voice down the hallway. It sounded as if someone was racing toward us. And then the clown was at the door, white shirt untucked, hair and eyes wild.

"Go, Stefon!" I said.

Whack! With a mighty blow, muscles bunching beneath his T-shirt, he split the wood. *Whack!* The second blow shook the cupola.

Cecilia darted past me, facing off with the clown, brandishing both screwdriver and wrench, darting and feinting around his tall, lanky frame.

I did my best to blockade Stefon, and keep both the clown and Cecilia away so he could work. Meanwhile, Elias Fuller was doing his best to get in Stefon's way, with Bunny grabbing at Elias, trying to get him away. Thank Goddess my sweetheart was unable to sense either of them.

"Ah Lam Wu!" I shouted, "you can show up anytime now! You know, pop on in! We can use your help."

The air swirled around me, and suddenly, the warlock was there.

"It's about time," I groused.

"We were searching! But I'm here now, and the others are on their way. Now," she said, head snapping around the already crowded cupola, "what is happening?"

"I think Cyrus is up there," I pointed, as Stefon kept whacking away, Cecilia stabbed at the clown, and Bunny and Elias kept fighting. At least the flapper had gotten the dead lumber baron away from Stefon, toward one of the open bays of the cupola.

What a mess.

Ah Lam Wu tilted her head as if listening.

"I think you're right," she said. "I sense Cyrus quite strongly here." And then she vanished. Just great. We were without backup. Again.

But not for long. I heard shouting and running up the stairs, then down the long hallway.

I turned to face the clown. His face was red with effort, anger, and confusion.

"What's your end game?" I blurted out. Great time to ask that question, Sarah.

"What?" He shook his head, still bobbing and weaving, smacking away Cecilia's screwdriver like a kid slapping at bees. That was a good sign. The clown could steal objects, and travel through space and time, but he didn't seem too good at fighting.

"You're asking me this now?" he said, huffing.

I shrugged. "Seems as good a time as any."

Whack! Whack!

"You almost through yet, Stefon?" I shouted over the clamor.

"Not yet!" he bellowed back, as if I wasn't standing two feet away. "Give me a minute!"

I heard pounding from overhead. At least I thought I did. Hard to tell with all the ax blows. Maybe it was Ah Lam Wu. Maybe it was Uncle Cyrus. I tried to open my senses, to get more information, but confusion boiled all around me. Between the fighting ghosts, the clown, the running, the pounding...

"Think, Sarah. Think. What do you need to know? What does Cyrus need you to know? What do the ghosts need you to know?" I whispered to myself, eyes half closed, seeking out my core. My center. My anchor. The seat of my magic.

Inhale. Exhale.

Whack! Whack!

There was something wrong. Something I hadn't picked up on yet. Something about Elias and the clown... Something Bunny, in her flighty, flapper way, had been pointing to.

The secret. The betrayal.

I looked at the clown. He looked back, face grimacing in pain, as if he was fighting something other than Cecilia.

I held out both of my hands, both to make myself larger, giving Stefon a little extra protection, but also because I needed everything to slow down. I needed everything to stop and to shift.

I saw it then. The thing I'd missed before. The shining cords that bound the clown to Elias Fuller. And it was definitely heading that direction: from the lumber baron to the clown.

Not the other way around. That's what the clown was fighting.

Other cords led away from the clown, growing faint and spindly the further out they went. Did they connect the clown to the ensorcelled rabbit?

Dang it! How had none of us picked up on this before? Elias Fuller must have been one heck of a powerful Masonic magician in life if he was powerful enough to control a human being after death.

At least, that's what the evidence was pointing to.

The tarot witch had been right. We had all been distracted. Bamboozled.

"Hecate!" I raised my voice, using the noise and confusion around me as a platform to lift my voice to the sky. "Hecate! Queen of magic! Bring your crossroads here! Hecate! Queen of magic! Lend me your power! Hecate! Queen of magic! Bring your torches here! Hecate! Queen of magic! In this fateful hour!"

The cupola rocked and swayed with the fighting, the ax blows, and the magic rising within me, pouring from my hands.

"Stop fighting me, you!" the clown screamed at Cecilia, who grinned and stabbed forward. The clown rocked backwards and I saw Raul grab him from behind, dragging his clown butt to the ground. The teens both sat on him.

Well, that was one way for a Goddess to answer my call.

Thank you, Hecate, I thought. Now what?

Bunny shrieked, her voice piercing my skull. And suddenly I knew. I was right. It had been Elias Fuller all along.

"Is the clown secured?" I asked.

"Just give me one. More. Sec." Raul's words punctuated his movements as he tied those lanky limbs with some cord from the toolbox. He glanced up at me, and flashed a smile. "I was a Boy Scout. Comes in handy."

I gave him and the teens a thumbs-up, then turned back to Stefon and the open Victorian bays of the cupola. The two ghosts still struggled in front of the gorgeous river view. Hecate, the queen of magic, had planted a whisper deep inside my head. A glimmer of ghost light and darkness. The sheen of candlelight on jewels. The image of men in elaborate aprons, acting out an ancient rite....

"Elias Fuller," I said, "you are guilty of conspiring to disrupt the Masonic Order and the sanctity of magic in this realm. You have sought to shore up your own power through greed, and you were using this one to do it." I jerked my head toward the now-subdued clown.

"And a rabbit!" Tracy said.

"And a rabbit," I agreed. "Elias Fuller, you were gathering elemental objects and...err...other things in order to secure your power on the astral planes, and to influence living members of the Masonic Order and other magic workers.

"Elias Fuller. I bind you."

::No!:: he shouted. ::*You cannot do this, witch! You have not got the power. I am the one....*::

"Elias Fuller. I bind you," I repeated a second time. The magic built inside me once again. The power of the Justice filled me. Bunny grappled with his arms, trying to hold him still. He still fought.

"Elias Fuller." My voice filled the cupola, roaring over the sound of Stefon's ax piercing wood. And the clown weeping and struggling on the floor.

I called on every scrap of magic that I could, raised both hands, and shoved the power toward the ghost.

"Elias Fuller. I bind you!"

With a great crack, the ceiling caved in, shards of wood crashing down. I raised my arms at the last minute, deflecting the blow, and staggered into Stefon. We fell towards the cupola's edge.

A hand grabbed my collar right before I tumbled three stories down. Ah Lam Wu.

Bunny and Elias Fuller were gone.

And my Uncle Cyrus lay in a heap on the broken boards, upon the cupola floor.

28

———

"Cyrus!" I rolled onto my knees, wincing. Everything hurt. I crawled to my uncle. Ah Lam was already crouched over him, tracing the palms of her hands over his ætheric bodies, checking for damage.

"Is he breathing?" I asked.

She nodded, lips pursed in concentration.

"You okay, babe?" Stefon's hand was warm on my shoulder. I leaned back into him for a moment, savoring the comfort of his scent and touch. No matter how badly things were going, being around Stefon managed to make me feel as if everything just might be okay.

"Where are the ghosts?" I croaked, then cleared my throat.

"They're not here?" Stefon looked around the damaged cupola.

I shook my head. Big mistake. An ache lanced its way through my right temple. I must've been hit on the head by one of the flying pieces of bead board. I looked up at the decimated ceiling.

Inscribed onto the panels holding up the cupola roof was a series of magical symbols. Must be Masonic. I recognized them from some of the artifacts in the rest of the building. I knew the old Masons were serious about infusing their buildings with power, but had still made the mistake of relegating Masons to a social club.

Wouldn't be doing that anymore.

"Oh my gosh!" Cecilia hovered over me, fuchsia hair damp with sweat, still clutching her mechanic's tools.

"Help me up?"

She dropped her tools with a clank, held out both hands, and pulled me to my feet.

Stefon rolled over and got to his knees without a groan. Guess getting smacked with broadswords for your hobby prepared your body for all sorts of abuse. He lurched to his feet and pulled me into a hug.

Broken boards creaked and crunched under my sneakers.

One good thing about dressing more casually than Ah Lam Wu and Uncle Cyrus? My jeans and T-shirt were much more appropriate for fighting and smashing up buildings.

We crunched our way over to Raul and the teens. They'd managed to drag the trussed-up clown back into the hallway, and none of them seemed worse for the wear.

Raul silently handed me a silver amulet on a broken chain.

I traced the pattern, recognizing the Masonic

square and compass in the midst of some filigree deco-ration. In the center of the symbol was an eye with rays around it.

"It broke when I grabbed him," Raul said.

At our feet, the clown groaned.

"What happened?" The clown blinked his eyes. "Where am I?"

He rolled a bit, and groaned some more. "And why am I tied up?"

The clown looked at me, brow furrowed in confusion and fear.

I bent down so I could get closer to him. I could tell that squinting up at me was taking a lot of effort, but dang, bending my knees hurt. Everything hurt.

"You're at the Fuller Mansion. Do you remember how you got here?"

He shook his head and his already pale face turn sheet white. Whoops.

"Can you all sit him up?"

The teens both nodded and gently propped the clown up.

"Take some deep breaths, okay?" Cecilia instructed. "Head between your knees."

He breathed in slowly. Deep, shaky, breaths.

"I don't understand what's happening...." He finally looked up and gestured feebly with his bound hands. "Who are you people?"

Whoa. This was seriously weird.

"What's the last thing you remember?" I asked. I felt Stefon hovering nearby, ready to pounce if the clown tried anything. I didn't blame my boyfriend, but my witchy senses told me this poor guy wasn't faking. I wasn't quite ready to untie him yet, though. Just in case.

"The last thing I remember?" he asked. "Yeah, it was here at the mansion. I'd been hired to entertain the kids at a Christmas party." He looked out across the cupola. I followed his gaze to the blue sky, the bridges, the river and downtown. The view in this open porch really was spectacular. Then he back at me. "Why is it sunny and warm out? It was cold. Pouring rain."

"I have bad news," I said. "I think a ghost was using you as a puppet and you've lost several months' time."

"I don't get it. How did this happen?" His voice rose in panic, and he started to shake.

I held up the amulet. "Do you remember this?"

"I don't think so...except. I think someone gave me a gift after I did my last set. A party favor..."

I scanned him with my psychic senses. The silver cords were gone.

I looked at Raul. "Untie him."

Cecilia shook her head and crossed her arms over her narrow chest.

Stefon scowled. "Sarah..."

"He's telling the truth," I said, standing up. "The amulet was controlling him. Besides, you, Raul, Tabitha, and Tracy are in charge of keeping tabs on him. We need to get him up, and then to a chair. Maybe get him some water."

"There's a sort of sitting room next door," Tracy offered.

"And I have a water bottle in my backpack," Tabitha added.

"All right," Stefon said, though he gave me one of those looks that told me he didn't like it.

I just shrugged, giving him a look back that said *We'll talk about this later.* It was handy, that kind of relationship communication, and frankly, it was really nice having someone I could do that with.

"I'll be in to ask some questions in a little bit," I said. "Thanks, you all."

"I don't feel right, leaving you alone," Stefon said, pausing. He had one of the clown's arms, supporting him, and Raul had the other.

Fine.

"Hey Raul," I said, "do you feel like you, Tracy, and Tabitha can take care of him and keep him safe?"

Raul leveled his eyes at me. Thinking. "We can do that. I'm pretty good at keeping people safe."

"I don't doubt that you are," I replied. Another conversation filled with subtext. This was getting a little weird, but better not to have this discussion in front of the clown. Even though I trusted that he was confused and had been used in this whole situation, there was still too much we didn't know.

"Okay handsome," I turned to my big, beautiful boyfriend. Huh. New acronym. BBB. "You can come with me. But I need to check in on Cyrus first."

"We should probably move him, too," Stefon replied. "To a more comfortable spot. That can't be good for him, lying on top of a bunch of broken boards." He tilted his chin toward my uncle and Ah Lam.

I had to admit he had a point.

"Can you carry him to one of the bedrooms down the hall?"

"Babe," he replied. "Of course I can."

I smirked. "You gonna start flexing now?"

He rolled his eyes at me and crunched his way back over the boards. I followed, lurching along as if I wasn't a multi-times-a-week jogger. What can I say? Beach sand is a lot easier to navigate than ceiling rubble.

"Hey, Uncle Cyrus." I crouched again, looking down at the face I knew and loved so well. Just like in my vision, there was a slight dusting of stubble on his head and chin, and sure enough, his shirt was torn. "Looks like you put up quite the fight."

His eyes fluttered, then opened. "Sarah?"

I clasped his left hand. "I'm here. And Stefon is going to help get you to a more comfortable place, okay?"

He frowned. "You have to find the ghosts. Elias Fuller…"

"We'll find him. It's okay. You just need to rest a bit, and we can compare notes later."

"But…"

"Sarah is right, Cyrus," Ah Lam said. Her words were soft, but lined with steel. Then she looked at Stefon. "I can pop him over."

Stefon nodded.

"All right, Cyrus, ready for a short trip?"

"I guess so," my uncle replied.

It almost broke my heart, seeing the warlock who had always been my mentor and champion laid so low.

But I also knew him well enough to know he wouldn't stay down for long.

I looked at Ah Lam.

"What's first? Questioning the clown, or tracking down Elias and Bunny?"

"Elias and Bunny," she said with no hesitation. "Right after I get your uncle moved.

I figured that would be her answer, but I didn't really like it.

29

The Victorian foyer was deserted. I followed the scent of wood fire back toward the library.

The space was hushed, almost stifling. As if the books, and rugs, and draperies blocked out the rest of the world. As if time itself had stopped. The only living thing in the room was the fire. And why hadn't I noticed before, how unusual it was for a fire to be burning in summer? I just took it as a piece with the historic nature of the mansion.

And maybe ghosts got cold.

Or perhaps time really had stopped here at that Christmas party, just as it had for the clown. Or maybe...

"Stefon?"

"Yeah babe?"

"Do you see a fire in the hearth?"

He furrowed his brow. "Fire? No. Why would there be a fire lit at this time of year? There's always a burn ban during summer. You know that."

I did know that. I'd just never seen a ghost fire before.

::Sarah.::

Bunny's voice prodded me back into the here and now.

"Where are you, Bunny?"

::Behind the bookcase nearest the door.::

"How many secret spaces does this place have?" I said, crossing the vast Persian carpet, skirting around the now-deserted tables. "And where did all the ghosts go?"

"What's happening?" Stefon asked, following me.

I began to push and pull on various books.

"Bunny says there is a secret room behind here. We just have to find the key."

He reached up and pushed on the wooden edge of the bookcase. With a snick, the case swung open an inch or two.

"How did you know?"

He shrugged. "You really need to play more video games and D&D. Always look for the thing that's out of place. It's the only knothole I saw, so I pushed it."

"Huh." I grabbed the edge of the bookcase and swung it toward me, revealing a slightly smaller, eight-walled room filled with magical artifacts, leather club chairs...

And ghosts.

"Bunny?" I asked. Stepping onto the jewellike carpet of the octangular room, I glanced back at Stefon, who was already looking around with admiration. "You should stick close to me. This place is full of ghosts."

His eyes widened slightly, but he nodded assent.

::*Over here,*:: Bunny replied.

I looked toward the far end of the room, and sure enough, there she was, standing next to a leather chair. In the chair was a very stiff Elias Fuller. The Masonic rake had strands of silver wrapped around his torso, arms, and legs.

My bindings. Cool. I'd never actually seen what they looked like before. I usually avoided binding people, on the supposition that it was better for energy to flow and change, rather than remain static. But sometimes in emergencies? Binding someone from causing more immediate harm became necessary.

Bunny held up a hand to indicate she'd be with me in a minute, then turned toward a tall man in a smoking jacket. He looked like Raul's brother, if Raul's brother was a dapper ghost.

::*Sarah Braxton?*::

I jumped. At my side was a buxom, middle-aged woman in a long, bronze-colored gown with a high neck, puffed upper sleeves that tightened just above the elbow, and elaborate embroidery down the front, ending in a V at her substantial, yet nipped-in waist. As another substantial woman, I loved the look of corsets, but for daily wear? No way. The hair piled on her head was also bronze, and a monocle covered her right eye.

If she hadn't smiled just then, I would have been seriously intimidated.

"I am," I replied, patting my hair, which was surely a snarled mess. I was suddenly conscious of my dirt-streaked, casual clothing. And who knew what my face looked like? Oh well. No help for it now. "And you are?"

::*My name is Agnes Aldworth. Did you bind Mr. Fuller?*::

I widened my stance and stood up tall, ignoring the ache in my lower back. "I did. Is that a problem?"

She gave me a wintry smile.

::Not at all. I wished to congratulate you on such a thorough job. The only problem is his perfidy.::

Well then.

"I have a man upstairs who appears to have been under Mr. Fuller's thrall. Mr. Fuller seemed to be using him to steal magical objects or objects meaningful to their owners in some way."

A flash of regret crossed her face. *::We suspected as much, but did not have enough proof to charge him.::*

"Sarah?" Ah Lam Wu's face popped around the edge of the open bookcase door. She stepped in. So did Uncle Cyrus. He looked terrible, but it was good to see him on his feet after what must have been quite the ordeal.

"And he trapped a warlock in the cupola upstairs." I said to the ghostly woman. As I spoke the words, I realized that this room must be the ground floor of that open cupola balcony. They were the same shape. This hidden room was the foundation of what was above.

"Is this room the seat of the mansion's magic?" I asked.

"It is," Ah Lam Wu said, stepping beside me. "It amplifies the magic that has lived in these halls for more than a century."

"Dang," Stefon said. "That's some powerful stuff."

I could tell he was taking internal notes for future gaming excursions. My big geek.

"Speaking of magic," I said, turning back to the Victorian ghost. "What do you know about this?"

I held out the amulet Raul had taken from the clown's neck.

::*The Eye of Providence within the square and compass. It can do many things, but is most often a reminder to Masons that the Great Architect watches over us all.*::

"Would it be a way for a magician to keep watch over a person?" Like, say, a clown they were controlling from afar?

She frowned. ::*That would be a terrible misuse of its power....*::

"But?" Uncle Cyrus asked. His voice was hoarse and sounded as terrible as he looked, currently leaning against the door jamb.

::*But it could be done.*::

"Okay," I said, tucking the amulet back into my pocket. I crossed my arms over my chest. "And about the cupola. How in the world did he trap someone there, and why didn't you do anything about it?"

The ghost stiffened, and an angry scowl crossed her face before she schooled them again.

"I think I can explain some of that," Uncle Cyrus said, stepping into the room. He swayed on his feet. I snapped my head toward the few chairs in the space. Most of the ghosts stood, but one particularly elderly-looking man sat, and a younger ghost perched on the arm of a second nearby chair.

"Stefon?" I said. "Would you bring Cyrus that chair?"

He propped his ax against one of the walls and headed for the chair. "It's empty?"

"Close enough."

Stefon sighed, but lifted the chair anyway, startling

the seated ghost, who winked out, then winked back in, three feet away, looking annoyed.

Tough.

We got Cyrus settled. I wanted nothing more than to draw him a bath and then get him to bed. But things had to be settled here, first.

"I came back to examine some of the artifacts, and see if I could pick up any clues about the missing ring in particular. It seemed strange to me that such a thing would be missing. It didn't quite match the other missing objects. And why one ring from here, when everything else was missing from Seashell Cove."

I shivered, despite the warmth of the room. Stefon placed an arm around me.

Cyrus cleared his throat.

"I realized all too late that I'd been lured into a trap." He raised his dark eyes to mine. "He was after you, Sarah. He wanted your power. That's why he sent that poor man to Seashell Cove, and started stealing things."

"And his ring?" I asked.

"Look," Cyrus said. We all turned toward the ghost of Elias Fuller. Sure enough, winking from his right hand was the ruby. "It was never missing. He just said it to get Ah Lam and me here."

"And we fell for it," the other warlock said, mouth tipped down in a frown.

::Elias can be very persuasive,:: Agnes Aldworth said. *::It made him a good Mason at first, his charm. But then it made him dangerous. He amassed great wealth and power during his lifetime, and, all these years after his death, decided he wanted another taste of it.::*

"What's happening?" Stefon murmured. "You're all just staring."

I squeezed his hand. "We're learning that Elias Fuller was a real jerk."

Stefon snorted. "I could've told you that."

"You could?"

"Of course. Don't you read history? All those lumber barons were jerks."

::*Excuse me,*:: Agnes said reprovingly. ::*May I continue?*::

"My apologies."

She harrumphed, but kept on with her explanation. ::*The symbols embedded in the cupola are strong enough to protect the mansion from outside magical attack, and Elias figured out a way to turn them so they could contain an outside magical being. We need to study exactly what he did, but that is the gist of it.*::

Wow. "And the objects?" I thought of Carol in particular, bereft without her athame. She had been hardest hit of everyone.

::*Are already en route back to their rightful owners. We have three ghosts working on it now.*::

"Okay then, with your permission, I think we'd better move this along. Do you want to sentence Mr. Fuller, or shall I?"

::*We ghosts shall do that,*:: she replied. ::*You have done enough.*::

I winced, thinking of the decimated cupola. "Yeah. Sorry about the cupola. But considering one of you trapped my uncle there, I can't say I wouldn't do it again if I needed to."

::*As well you should,*:: she said, sternly, then trained

her eyes on Uncle Cyrus. *::We owe you a boon for the terrible treatment you have received at the hands of one of our own. Call upon us if you have need of anything. And all of you, feel free to visit the mansion and study our artifacts.::*

"That is most gracious of you," Ah Lam Wu said.

The ghost inclined her head in acknowledgement.

Bunny finally approached, beaded frock swinging, having finished her conversation.

::Sarah, I am so sorry you got messed up with this cad.::

"It's all in a day's work, Bunny. But I'm sorry you did, too."

::Can I come back with you all? I don't think I can bear to stick around this mausoleum.::

"There's always room for you," I said. And, surprisingly, given what a pain in the butt the flapper had been, I meant it.

30

———

The garden was beautiful. My neighbor's sunflowers poked their sunny heads over the fence, and water glinted off my little slice of the Pacific Ocean down below. My feet were propped up, I had a glass of Vino Verde in one hand—courtesy of Uncle Cyrus—and Stefon held my other as he sipped a local beer. Ah Lam Wu and Uncle Cyrus sat across the table from us, both dressed down by virtue of not wearing blazers and rolling up the sleeves of their starched dress shirts.

Two peas in a pod. I hoped the something that was brewing between them stuck. I liked Ah Lam Wu.

Rhiannon had consented to come home with me, and stalked the edges of the garden, looking for who knows what.

It was the calm between storms as we waited for the rest of the partygoers to arrive.

It had been a busy week in Seashell Cove. I had given Duncan a couple of days off, and the teens had completely revamped The Widening Gyre website and started a new social media campaign.

The Rabbit Brothers, as I'd taken to calling them, had been hanging around some, as had Ash and Jerry Hamamoto. The clown—turns out his name was Ivan—had let them keep the rabbit on one condition: that they called her Eva instead of Chuckles. The boys both agreed.

"Hello!" Cecilia called back. "Whole bunch of weirdos heading on back!"

"Come on through, weirdos!" I called, face splitting into a grin.

And here they were, my ragtag community. My closest friends. The people who, I was discovering, were sticking by my side through thick and thin.

Cecilia and Toby, mismatched and in love, arms filled with fruit from Toby's garden and what smelled like freshly baked bread. Raul, carrying a six-pack. Tabitha, Tracy, and Carol, arms filled with grocery bags. Delta Crabbit and Preston the gnome, the latter of whom immediately ran over to see what Rhiannon was doing.

And lastly, tentatively, Ash, Jerry Hamamoto, and Ivan the clown.

Ivan still looked a bit shell-shocked, and Jerry looked at me as if I might bite. I set my glass down on the table and rose to greet them.

"Welcome to my Seashell Cove Summer Case Solved party! Thank you for coming."

I looked at Jerry and Ivan. "Really. I'm glad you're here. There are cups, plates, and napkins on the back porch, and plenty of chairs. Please make yourselves at home."

Ivan slid his lanky frame into a chair near Uncle Cyrus. He wore jeans and a "Magic Happens" T-shirt today, but still had on his telltale black sneakers with the red stripe. Ash and the teens went to pester Preston and Rhiannon.

"Carol?" I asked, as the blond witch pulled her chair closer. "How are you feeling?"

She looked much better. The shadows had left her eyes and it seemed as if she'd actually gotten some sleep.

"Relieved," she said. "Having my athame gone was…"

"Like losing a piece of yourself?" Ah Lam asked.

Carol nodded. "I packed it in salt all week to cleanse it, and took it out for ritual last night."

"And?" I asked.

She smiled at me, lighting up like the westering sun.

"It was great. Perfect."

Jerry Hamamoto cracked open one of Raul's beers and Toby and Cecilia moved in closer, too. Despite the sun and warmth, everyone clearly wanted to feel the connection that came from sitting practically shoulder to shoulder in a circle.

If I didn't know better, I'd say they were acting like a coven of witches, ready to celebrate the turning of the sun. For a moment, I allowed myself to wonder what that would feel like. To have a group of people to do magic with on a regular basis, instead of just in the midst of crisis.

I looked at Carol, and Jerry, and Delta. And at Tracy and Tabitha, too. I didn't know what the future held yet, but there was definitely something there.

"Lost in thought, babe?" Stefon asked.

I raised his hand to my lips for a kiss.

"Just thinking how good it feels to be relaxing among friends. And to know that everyone is safe." At least for now.

Jerry cleared his throat. "I was wondering..."

"What's that?" I asked.

"Do you think you could give Ash some training? Having some friends seems to be calming him down...." He looked at the teens and Ash, laughing as Rhiannon and Preston chased each other around a clump of bushes. "He likes the two brothers and the rabbit, and those two girls have been really good for him."

"But he needs more," Uncle Cyrus said. "Every magic worker needs some structured training to get their gifts under control."

Jerry sighed. "Yes. And I've been failing miserably at it."

"Don't be so hard on yourself," Ah Lam chimed in, taking a sip of her wine. "Sometimes parents are the right mentors, but other times its better to have someone outside the family unit for support. Especially when times have been hard."

"Kind of like you trained me," I said to Cyrus. "I mean, sure, you're family even though we aren't related, but sometimes I needed someone who wasn't Mom or Dad around."

Jerry looked relieved. "You mean its not just me?"

Everyone around the table laughed.

"Come on, man," Raul said. "I don't know much about all this magic stuff, except from hanging out with this crew on occasion, but it's the same all over. Kids need outside influences sometimes. Blood family is too close. Stifling, you know?"

"He's right," Carol said. "It's why Tabitha's parents let her spend so much time with me, and why I want Tracy to get outside training, too."

"Makes sense," Jerry replied. "Thanks. So at any rate, Sarah, Ash and I would appreciate the help."

I looked at Uncle Cyrus, so grateful he was back to his usual debonair self. "We've been talking about structuring a proper apprenticeship with the teens anyway. What's one more?"

"To always making room for one more," Cecilia said, raising her beer.

We all toasted to that, and drank.

"And I'm hoping you'll help, too, Delta," I said.

She snorted. "If you really want my help, you know you've got it."

"Jerry," Toby said, voice quiet as always. The hob leaned forward. "I'm always happy for Ash to come hang out at our house, too. I could teach him kitchen and garden stuff if he's interested. And...it might do him good to be around someone a little bit like him."

Jerry had tears in his eyes as he reached a hand out toward the hob. "Thank you, Toby. That would be great."

We sat and drank in silence for a few moments, letting the conversation settle around us. Finally Rhiannon sauntered over and leapt up onto my lap. I scratched her head. Preston climbed up next to Delta on her chair, Ash leaned against his dad, and the two teens pulled up a garden bench and plopped down, in the boneless way only teenagers seem able to pull off.

"Jerry?" I asked.

"Hmm?"

"Would you mind giving us a reading?"

His face lit up. "I would like to do nothing more."

Pulling his velvet sack from his backpack, he drew out the well loved deck of cards.

"Everyone reach your hands out toward the cards and imagine one wish you have, right now."

::*Do I have to do this, too?*:: Rhiannon asked.

"If you want your wish to come true, you do," I replied.

She held out a paw.

I noticed Ivan was crying. "You okay, Ivan?"

"I'm great. I've just never felt this connected to other people before. And I'm so glad to be back in this world."

I nodded, and held out my hand, sending a small burst of energy, along with my wish, toward the cards.

Jerry closed his eyes, and cut the deck three times. Then he laid out three cards.

"In the past, we have the Seven of Cups. Delusion and illusion."

Well, we certainly had all been through that. Elias Fuller had put a whammy on us all.

"In the present? The Sun."

"What's the future, dad?" Ash asked.

Jerry's grin split his face.

"The Three of Cups. Collaboration. Celebration. And friendship."

"To friendship!" Ash said, bouncing on his toes.

We all raised our hands to toast again.

"To friendship!"

And to many more magical days to come.

*F*ootnote: *Want to find out how Sarah learned Rhiannon can talk? Check out* Rhiannon and the Queen of Cats *in the collection* Cats and Other Creatures, *available March, 2022.*

*M*eanwhile... *what's next?*

Sarah is in training for the annual Wag More Charity Run in Seashell Cove, but something has gone terribly wrong.

Even Rhiannon is worried...

Find out what happens next, in **Running Witch**, *available May, 2022.*

T. THORN COYLE
AUTHOR OF THE WITCHES OF PORTLAND
RUNNING WITCH
A SEASHELL COVE
PARANORMAL MYSTERY

ACKNOWLEDGMENTS

Thank you to Chris and Bonnie for checking my cozy levels early in the process! Thanks to Leslie and Jack for reading, to Dayle for editing, and to Robert and Jonathan for years of support. Thanks to Dean and Loren for Kickstarter help.

And speaking of which, thank you to the 324 people who took a chance on my paranormal cozies for freaks and geeks. I'm speechless with gratitude for the support!

Most of you are listed below. For those anonymous ones who wanted no credit? Well, Rhiannon and Sarah know who you are.

A big, Kickstarter thank you to:

Abigail M. Fellnor, Adrian Emerson, Ahmarah, Aahzmandius, Alesia, Alexandra O'Bryan, Alison Naomi Holt, Allie Gentry, Alyson, Amara Snively, Ambar, Amy Montarbo, Andréa María, Angela Rain-catcher, Anna McCluskey, Anne E. Lynch, Annelise F.M., Annie Reed, Aramanth, Arianne, Becca, Becca K., Bonnie Elizabeth, Book Bunny, Breann Carpenter, Bookwyrmkim, Brad Snyder, Brendan "HollyKing" Leber, Brendon Reece, Bridgette Findley, Brooke Pratt,

Carey Oxler, Carol, Carolyn Rowland, Carrie Boon, Cate Kneale, Catherine, Catriona, Céline Malgen, Bryn Hofmann, Celine, Charlie Boehme-Byrd, Chassidy Strege, Cheryl Hammond, C. F Linnds, Chris Kaiser, Chris Paton, Christina Terhune, Cintia De Carvalho, CJ, Claire Manning, Claudia Nymphenkuss, CM Wolf, Colby Smith, Constance, Crystal, Dagmar Baumann, DL, Daniel J. Riddle, David H Hendrickson, Dawn McMorrow, Dayle Dermatis, Deanna Stanley, Debbie Mumford, Deb Bodeau, Deft, Della Keeley, Diana Deverell, Diane M Smith, Dianne M. Daniels, Diva Style Minister, E., E. Scott, E Dimopoulos, Efoy, Emily Pedersen, Emily, Emma Shelford, Enfys Book, Eric & Carla Chamberlin, Erin, Erin Ratelle, Erin, Faerie Sarah, Felicia Fredlund, Fennec Foxfire, Gemma, Georgette Paxton, Gertjan, GhostCat, Glenda Nowakowski, Goldie, Greenraven, Gwells, Hal, Hannah Golden, Heidi Moone, Helen Bridget Adeline Eastwood, Helen Hawk, Henry Espy Roberts, H Alexander Perez, Hobbit, Holly, Honoré Artaud, Imani J Dean, Inanna Hazel, Amy Laurens, Iris, Ivo Dominguez Jr, Izzy Hanelt, JK, Jim Gotaas, Jamie Forster, Janet Ní Shúilleabháin, Janette Fletcher, Janine Cobb, jaymi elford, Jeanna, Jeannine, JS Groves, Jenett, Jennifer Beltrame, Jennifer Bramhill, Jennifer, Jennifer Forness, Jennifer Mroz, Jessica F, Jessica Johansen, Jessica Marquardt, Jess Werner, Jinx, JoAnn, Johanna Rothman, John Bell, John Deltuvia, John W. Luther, Jon Auerbach, Jonathan Korman, Joe Cleary, Jaeelle Hayes, Julia Levine, Kajtryna, Karen Dougherty, Karen Snodgrass, Kat Humphries, Kate Pavelle, Kathryn F, Katina Clarke, Katy Manck – BooksYALove, Kaye & Sand, Kelly

Chang, Ken Irwin, Kendall B, Kerry Paolucci, Kickstarter Music, Kim Z, Kirsten M. Corby, Kri O'Kellas, Kristen Gehrke, Kristin Rollins, Ladypants, Lanette Miller, LaRena Rose, L. E. Knight, Leslie Claire Walker, Lezlie Revelle Zucker, Lilith, Liluri, Lily Wolthers, Lindsay DelGrosso, Lisa Costello, Lisa Sanger Blinn, Lora Shimer, Loren L Coleman, Lorelei Sherman, LaffingKat, Louisa Swann, Louise Lieb, Leigh Saunders, Mackensey S, Maddie, Maggie Fry, Mambo Chita Tann, Mar Azul, Margaret, Margit Hofmann, Marian Phillips, Marine Lesne, Marissa Schwartz, MoonCrone, Mark Carter, Mary Jo Rabe, MaryAnne, Matt Fabian, Maya Kate, Megan Potter, Merri Anne Stowe, M.G. Herron, Meyari McFarland, Michael Warren Lucas, Michelle Bryant Barbeau, Michelle Mishmash, Minkenstein, MJ Silversmith, Monica Van Steenberg, Morpheus Ravenna, Myke Johnson, Karen Fonville, name, Nancy Sloop, Nate Hernandez-Botma, Nathania Apple, Neil Coles, Niall Gordon, Nicole Lynch, Nicolina, Odd, Oliver Peltier, OwlLight, Phoebe Miller, pjk, Polly, POTU David, Author, Purple Steam Dragon, Quinn Kelly, R. Hunter, Rachel Peterson, Raven Cornelius, Rebecca Hiatt, Renee Rice, R.S. Kellogg, Rebecca M. Senese, Roxan, Richard A. Loftus, Richard Hoffman, River Roberts, Rob Vagle, Robin Hill, Rosalynde, Rrrose, Ru Temple, Ruth Wotton, Ryan M. Williams, Sage, Sage Cara, SallyRose Robinson, Samantha Landstrom, Sanchini Family, Sandra Choate, Sandra H, Sandra Mueller, Sanguine Kitty, Sara Blackthorne, Sara Ontiveros, Sarah, Sarah Underwood, Sarah A., Sarah Clark, Sea, Sea Queen, Shannon Davis, Sharon H, Sharon Rowse, Silke, Sioux Rowan, Skayle Bloodwomon, Sky Fowler, Simone P., Somcak, Sophia, soul-jacker85, Steph Wetch, Stephen VanWambeck, Stephanie Longoria, Stephen Ballentine, Steven Whitacre, Steve Locke, Sunshine, Susanne Winter, Tasha Turner, Taylor Morich, Teri Moody, Thalassa, Thea Hutcheson, Thealandrah, Tina, T.L. Merrybard, Tony Malerich, Tony Rella, Tracy Eire, Two renegade Appalachians, Tyler Spencer, Visucien Fe, Valerie Herron, Valkyrie, Victoria S., Violet Twilight, Wendy Williamson, Will Gwaltney, Yuu Gamon

ABOUT THE AUTHOR

T. Thorn Coyle has worked in several strange and diverse occupations. Buy them a cup of tea and perhaps they'll tell you about it.

Author of the *Seashell Cove Paranormal Mystery* series, *The Steel Clan Saga*, *The Witches of Portland*, and *The Panther Chronicles*, Thorn's multiple non-fiction books include *Sigil Magic for Writers, Artists & Other Creatives*, and *Evolutionary Witchcraft*.

Thorn's work appears in many anthologies, magazines, and collections. They have taught magical practice in nine countries, on four continents, and in twenty-five states.

An interloper to the Pacific Northwest U.S., Thorn stalks city streets, writes in cafes, loves live music, and talks to crows, squirrels, and trees.

Connect with Thorn:
www.thorncoyle.com

ALSO BY T. THORN COYLE

FICTION

The Panther Chronicles (Complete)

To Raise a Clenched Fist to the Sky

To Wrest Our Bodies From the Fire

To Drown This Fury in the Sea

To Stand With Power on This Ground

The Witches of Portland (complete)

By Earth

By Flame

By Wind

By Sea

By Moon

By Sun

By Dusk

By Dark

By Witch's Mark

The Steel Clan Saga

We Seek No Kings

We Heed No Laws

We Ride at Night

Seashell Cove Paranormal Mysteries

Bookshop Witch

Haunted Witch

Tarot Witch

Running Witch

Short Story Collections

A Hint of Faery

A Touch of Faery

A Spark of Magic

A Flame for Yuletide

A Hope for Winter

A Speculation of Stars

A Speculation of Hope

Risk It All: Queer Stories of Love, Suspense, And Daring

Thresholds: Queer Stories of Love, Suspense, And Daring

Non-Fiction

Evolutionary Witchcraft

Kissing the Limitless

Make Magic of Your Life

Sigil Magic for Writers, Artists & Other Creatives

Crafting a Daily Practice